THOMAS HOLLEY CHIVERS

Nacoochee
(1837)

By Thomas Holley Chivers

A FACSIMILE REPRODUCTION
WITH AN INTRODUCTION BY
CHARLES M. LOMBARD

SCHOLARS' FACSIMILES & REPRINTS
DELMAR, NEW YORK, 1977

Published by
Scholars' Facsimiles & Reprints, Inc.
Delmar, New York 12054

New matter in this edition
©1977 Scholars' Facsimiles & Reprints, Inc.
All rights reserved

Printed in the United States of America

Library of Congress Cataloging in Publication Data

Chivers, Thomas Holley, 1809–1858.
Nacoochee: 1837.

Reprint of the 1837 ed.
Printed by W.E. Dean, New York.
I. Title.
PS1294.C4N3   1977   811'.3   77-24233

ISBN 0-8201-1295-X

INTRODUCTION

From 1837 to 1842 Chivers, with the exception of a few trips down South, spent most of his time in the North in the general vicinity of New York. It marked a long period away from Georgia and proved to be a productive one for he published a major volume of poetry. As was usually the case he paid a printer, W. E. Dean, 2 Ann Street, New York, to publish the work in 1837 under the title *Nacoochee; or, The Beautiful Star, with Other Poems.* Although the preface is dated September 10, 1837, S. Foster Damon notes that one of the poems has the date of October, 1837, when revised and printed in a later volume. This gives rise to two possibilities. Either Chivers forgot the date when *Nacoochee* was published or else the preface was written some time before the actual date of publication.

In the main *Nacoochee* shows definite improvement over previous works, *The Path of Sorrow* and the play, *Conrad and Eudora* which included a section of short lyrics entitled *Songs of the Heart.* The volume has value as evidence of an important step in Chivers' poetic development. He exercises considerable restraint, is more careful in use of language and meter, and still displays sufficient inventiveness to experiment with words in the hope of expanding the vocabulary of poetry. There are signs of his reading of Keats and Shelley but the prevailing tone is inescapably Chiversian. For better or for worse the cantankerous Georgian had his own unique turn of phrase and poetic pattern. Frequently the results were banal but on more than one occasion in *Nacoochee* the reader meets with lines of singular beauty and harmony.

The prefaces to Chivers' works are important since they contain comments on his esthetic views and the one to *Nacoochee* is especially interesting for already there is evidence of the Swedenborgian elements entering into the formulation of his poetics. Chivers had been a fervent Baptist

v

and he retained his evangelical zeal after embracing the tenets of the New Church. Through the theory of correspondence Swedenborg opened to Chivers fresh poetic vistas. The universe was alive with symbols, not mere abstractions but reminders of a higher order of truths in the World of Spirits. So when Chivers speaks in the preface of the "anticipation of the enjoyment of the fellowship of angels in that other intellectual world" he is not merely uttering some shopworn Platonic commonplace. His poems abound with references to angelic presences in man's midst, a reminder of the Swedenborgian precept that the next life is just a step away. When man abandons the material body the spiritual body remains. In fact, it is with the spiritual ears and eyes that the Georgian poet hears and beholds sounds and colors that correspondentially link him immediately to supernal verities.

Unmistakably in the preface to *Nacoochee* Chivers, already strongly affected by Swedenborgianism, is seeking an ecstatic form of poetic experience akin to mystic exaltation. It was this very aspect of this poetic view that separated him from Poe and the rest of his contemporaries. Chivers cast himself in the role of the Romantic poet-prophet with the two-fold mission of spreading the new poetics and the gospel of Swedenborg. Little wonder that practically no one understood him in his lifetime. Today there is still little interest in Chivers' religious message but the Georgian's poetic theory is engrossing to students of the history of literature. Several decades before the French Symbolists he conceived of the sonic quality of words superseding their traditional function of conveying meaning alone. Music and poetry in Chivers' mind shared a common goal, namely, the organization of beauty towards sound. "It is the outpourings of the skies, and the crystal rivers of the fountain of religion." Convinced of the oneness of poetic and mystic experience, Chivers selected the seashell as a metaphor of physical existence that contains the echo of eternity. The reverberations produced by the shell held to the ear reflected in a small way the poet's awareness of and proximity to a higher order of revelation.

Besides Swedenborg Chivers was strongly attracted to

Chateaubriand. In the first half of the nineteenth century
the elegant French Romantic's *Atala* affected the thinking of
American poets focusing attention on the Indian as a subject
for poetry. Although well acquainted with the aborigine's
good and bad points they still preferred to visualize the
redman as an untainted son of nature cast in the mold of
Atala and Chactas, the lovers in Chateaubriand's prose idyl.
Chivers claimed he based the title poem *Nacoochee* on an
Indian legend common among tribes dwelling in the South
but in reality he is endebted to Chateaubriand for much of
the poem's atmosphere and symbolism. Chivers wrote short
poems based on scenes and themes taken directly from *Atala*
and longer poems as well. The Georgian was entranced by
Chateaubriand's depiction of an Indian maid who united in
her person the pristine charm and freshness of the aborigine
with the grace and poise of a young girl patterned after the
elegant European models then current in fiction. Unquestion-
ably the story line of "Nacoochee" is a standard Romantic
plot of European origin. The boy-girl relationship was rel-
atively unknown in Indian legend. Alleged stories of two
Indian lovers and the death-leap are contrivances of white
writers and totally foreign to the real spirit of Indian mythol-
ogy. Ostenee, the young brave who sets out in search of the
beautiful Nacoochee is for all intents and purposes Chateaubriand's Chactas seeking the hand of the elusive and enig-
matic Atala. In Chateaubriand's tale the ill-advised heroine
takes her own life to remain true to a vow made to her
mother never to have carnal relations with a man. Chivers
uses the basic theme of the French author's prose romance,
sublimates the original motif, and places it on a higher
spiritual plane to exemplify a more exalted and purified
ideal. Whereas Atala does kiss and embrace Chactas, Chivers permits no physical contact whatsoever between his
two principals. In the preface Chivers tells us that the young
brave, Ostenee, "falls in love with one of those celestial
beings"; obviously this is a European literary convention
transplated rather awkwardly to semi-civilized environs and
to a less sophisticated culture. For all its artifices *Atala* is
far more successful as a French transplant in the American
wilderness, thanks to Chateaubriand's superb prose style.

This is not to say that Chivers was unaffected by the sensuous and luxuriant atmosphere of Chateaubriand's descriptions, some of which were retained in the English translation of *Atala* used by Chivers.

In the preface Chivers promises a sequel to "Nacoochee" which subsequently appeared in the poem *Atlanta* in 1853, some sixteen years later. Here the two chief figures of *Atlanta*, Julian and Ianthe, are members of the white establishment dressed as aborigines. Their refined emotions and reactions are reminiscent of Atala and Chactas. Julian and Ianthe consummate their reunion in the most sensual manner, a far cry from the chaste standards set by Nacoochee. Subsequently they sublimate their baser drives and attain the sort of angelic state that in Swedenborgianism is a harbinger of the celestial perfection enjoyed in heaven. Chivers seems to have cherished the notion of a Swedenborgian Indian in whom the pristine freshness and ingenuousness of the aborigine would be combined with the spiritual perfection attainable through the precepts of the New Church. The theme of Edenic man, as he existed in the Garden of Eden, is a leitmotiv in Chivers' scattered statements on esthetics found throughout his prefaces to published works and in manuscripts. "Nacoochee" and *Atlanta* best exemplify his notion of Edenic man as a poetic theme inspired by Chateaubriand and Swedenborg.

Other poems in *Nacoochee* owe at least part of their inspiration to Chivers' reading of Chateaubriand. The Georgian's paean of the Mississippi, "Thus endless, majestic, supreme, and divine/" captures some of the solemnity of the opening pages of *Atala* with its striking word-portrait of the Father of Waters. (Harriet Beecher Stowe was so captivated by Chateaubriand's impressions of the Mississippi that she inserted a quotation from the preface to *Atala* right in the middle of *Uncle Tom's Cabin!*) "Nacoochee's Prayer" is strongly reminiscent of the pious effusions of Atala on her deathbed after deliberately taking poison to avoid physical union with Chactas in obedience to the oath extracted from her by a fanatical mother; Nacoochee addresses the Christian deity as Abba, an Aramaic term for God the Father. Unlike Atala Nacoochee at all times is in complete control of her spiritual destiny and when in danger of being approached by Ostenee is miraculously borne away by Azrael, the angel in Jewish and Islamic angelology who separates the soul from the body at the moment of death. Select souls in Swedenborg's tradition are at times supernaturally borne away in chariots by angels. (Chivers also adds here a touch of his own theological syncretism.)

"The Burial of the Indian Child" is another scene directly from *Atala* although the sorrowful words are Chivers' with all their maudlin yet tender quality. The squaw holding the dead child is called Lena. (Chivers confused time and again Ossianic terminology in *Atala* with Indian nomenclature with occasionally bizarre effects.) "Neah-Emathlah," although based on an actual incident in Jackson's warfare with the Creeks, contains nonetheless some typical Chateaubriandesque features in the noble language, sentiments, and stoicism of the captured chieftain.

"Malavolti; or, the Downfall of the Alamo" is the worst poem in the collection and the elements borrowed from *Atala* only serve to underscore its ridiculousness. The title character Malavolti, is a fickle lover. His first love, an Indian maid (with the Ossianic name, Lena, again) dies only to return in ghostly form in several scenes patently taken from *Atala*; Chivers apparently was fascinated with those passages where Chateaubriand pictured Atala appearing in the moonlight to frighten superstitious braves. Another aboriginal lass, Naymoyah, an additional borrowing from Chateaubriand's list of Indian names, comes under Malavolti's spell only to be warned in the nick of time by Lena's ghost. Unfortunately Chivers received no such friendly admonition before composing "Malavolti."

Chivers' penchant for confusing Ossianic and Indian names is explainable in part by Chateaubriand's frequent references to Macpherson's writings and the names of some of the characters appearing in them. Given the Georgian's rather odd sense of proportion, to say the least, he was quite capable of joining Celtic and Indian appelations with wild abandon. Chivers also had his own peculiar views on philology and the origin of language expressed flamboyantly and vociferously in *Search After Truth,* an indispensable

work for any serious student of the Georgian. Another ex-
planation for the juxtaposition of Celtic and Indian names
may be found in the current "Welsh Theory" to which even
some soberminded scholars then gave credence. This hypo-
thesis, discredited long since, maintained that before Col-
umbus Welsh sailors crossed the Atlantic during the early
part of the Middle Ages, landed in America, and settled
down among the Indians. Occasionally in Colonial days some
missionary of Welsh background would report on unexpected
meeting with Indians who spoke the language of Wales.

Chivers' preoccupation with the American Indian as suit-
able subject matter for poetry persisted. Two plays in man-
uscript, *Count Julian* and *Osceola*, attest to his continued
interest in poetry based on the redman. He even once in-
sisted that Longfellow stole the meter for *Hiawatha* from
him. Be that as it may, *Nacoochee* with the graceful lyricism
and the haunting sonority of its best passages ranks as one
of the noteworthy examples of American poetry inspired by
the Indian and one of the more successful attempts to
capitalize on the Atala theme during the early period of
American Romanticism in the United States.

The Georgian poet's fascination with the Indian was an
integral part of his regionalism for Chivers was deeply in-
volved with several phases of the culture of his native Georgia. He had a strong affinity to the folklore of both the white
yeomanry and the slaves. His renditions of black work songs
and religious chants are probably the first worthwhile ver-
sions recorded by a white poet. Interspersed through *Nacoochee* there are poems imbued with his love of the Georgian
soil and his simple evangelical faith. Some of Chivers' best
moments occur when he gives free rein to his folkloric bent.
Then joyful and unaffected lines with a charming melody
flow easily from his pen. In many of the hymn books of the
period secular tunes could be found in the same volume with
religious songs. Among the commentaries in these hymnals
occasional reference was made to the importance of sim-
plicity and tunefulness in composing a melody. Accustomed
to a freer tradition of congregational hymn singing in the
Baptist Church Chivers may have first acquired there some
of his notions on the interrelation of poetry and music.

Readers wishing to acquaint themselves with this facet of
Chivers' work should read with particular attention poems
like "Evening," "Song of Adoration to God," "Song—Georgia
Waters," and "Ode to the Mississippi."

Although reared in a dour Baptist tradition Chivers was
not averse to treating bacchanalian motifs. Several poems in
Nacoochee suggest more than a nodding acquaintance with
Thomas Moore. Himself a tee-totaler Chivers had no com-
punction about composing an occasional poem on the de-
lights of alcoholic conviviality. "Drink and Away" was not
inspired by a communion service.

The high rate of child mortality that plagued the nineteenth century always was a persistent topic in Chivers'
verse. A loving father, he lost several of his own children
and the death of nieces and nephews as well as the offspring
of friends also affected him deeply.

Two poems in *Nacoochee* that usually excite the admira-
tion of critics are "The Death of Time" and "The Soaring
Swan." The former may owe something in theme and title to
The Course of Time (1827) by Robert Pollak (1798-1827). Any
similarity stops there. Chivers' penetration into the highest
realms of abstraction in non-temporality is an absorbing
poetic venture. The non-sensory is depicted sharply and
impressively in sensual terms. A similar effect is achieved
in "Nacoochee" where the Indian maid's physical allure is
translated into terms of spiritual purity. The image of the
"grave of Time" being "dug by Angels" is Chivers' challenge
to the advocates of material symbols as the sole source of
poetic metaphors.

"The Soaring Swan" with its visionariness and deft use of
chiaroscuro has prompted James A. Harrison and S. Foster
Damon to speculate that Rossetti not only was familiar with
Chivers' poem but was influenced by it. There may well be
Pre-Raphaelite facets to "The Soaring Swan" but the poem's
wider significance is lost in merely considering its possible
relationship to Rossetti. Magazine poetry of the time in America is replete with inconsequential attempts to capture in
verse the glorious expanses of the continent's unspoiled and
majestic wilderness. What is witnessed in "The Soaring
Swan" is one of the first successful efforts to pay tribute in

lyric form to the breath-taking beauty of nature revealed in all its magnificence in America of the early nineteenth century. As the swan soars so does Chivers' spirit. To him the bird might well symbolize the Paraclete. "Bathed in the fleecy bankments of the sky" the swan enables Chivers to pour out effortlessly his fascination with the heavens and space. Seldom has his visuality been displayed with such spontaneity and unbounded joy. He ventilates his enthusiasm for a nature that reflects his profound spiritual longings. Is the swan on wing a foretoken of the flight of Chivers' soul one day to the celestial spheres depicted by Swedenborg? Not an overdrawn assumption, it would appear, in light of Chivers' intensely religious disposition.

Theology, however, in Chivers' poetry was seldom a hindrance. If anything, his obsession with Swedenborg awakened him to the poetic possibilities of the world about him. We know from his unpublished comments on esthetics that he beheld in the universe an endless chain of symbols all directly linked to the ultimate Beauty of which God alone is the exemplar. The present reprint edition of *Nacoochee* supplies valuable data about an important stage of Chivers' development and delineates the steps that led to the moments of unique and indefinable expression in *The Lost Pleiad, Eonchs of Ruby,* and *Virginalia.*

CHARLES M. LOMBARD

University of Illinois at Chicago Circle

NACOOCHEE;

OR,

THE BEAUTIFUL STAR,

WITH

OTHER POEMS.

BY T. H. CHIVERS, M.D.

Break forth into joy, Sing!—*Isaiah.*

The fountains of our deepest life, shall be
Confused in passion's golden purity,
And we will talk, until thought's melody
Become too sweet for utterance.—*Epipsychidion.*

NEW YORK:

W. E. DEAN, PRINTER, 2 ANN STREET.

1837.

DEDICATED

TO

MY PRECIOUS MOTHER,

Who is the fountain of my existence, and the nourisher of my childhood—who is the cherisher of my life, and the sustainer of my hopes—who is the kindest of all that is kind, and the dearest of all that is dear—who has nursed me in her arms, and fed me at her breast—who loves me better than all love, except my love for her ; these poems are affectionately inscribed, by her devoted son, THE AUTHOR.

PREFACE.

POETRY is that crystal river of the soul which runs through all the avenues of life, and after purifying the affections of the heart, empties itself into the Sea of God. Now, he who dives the deepest into that mysterious sea, brings up the greatest number of the shells of truth, and is made richer in the lore of the wisdom of the universe. For, the more a man sees of the wise relations that subsist between him and God, the greater number of the strings of joy does he touch, because he is thereby made capable of diving deeper into the perfections of the things that are, and of communing oftener with the Author of those several beauties. It is, therefore, evident, that the more we investigate the relations that subsist between us and the Creator, the more are our minds expanded, affections matured, and the more are our hopes enlarged in the anticipation of the enjoyment of the fellowship of angels, in that other intellectual world, where happiness survives alone, and where we shall assume those beautiful conformities to God, of which we only dream in this. It is also evident, that, as we have implanted within us, a moral principle of right and wrong—what will benefit us, and what will not—to suffer the advancement of our minds to become sterile, in the contemplation of those things, is to degrade the loftiness of our nature, and trample

a

upon the highest privileges bestowed upon us by the Creator. If we possess faculties unbounded in their nature—deep and unfathomable in their purity—faculties which are capable of thirsting continually for the healing wells of life—we must infer that there are joys in heaven, as far above our aspirations in this world, as our thoughts are acclimated above our petty passions and subordinate desires. It is also evident, that, if the soul of man is so constituted, from the nature of its infinity, that it cannot be satisfied with any thing in this world, it must also follow that there must be a resting-place for it in another state of existence, proportionate to the magnitude of its desires in this.

Poetry is the power given by God to man of manifesting these relations. It is that wave of the soul, in the ocean of life, which washes the shores of the flower-gemmed Elysium. It is that beacon of joy upon the Utopian Isles, which ushers us into, the realities of those things which are to be. It is only the susceptible, poetical, and refined mind that can see these things as they are, while others think they only see them as they ought to be.

But that exalted inspiration which a man breathes as he quaffs the wellsprings of the universe, is different from that divine efflux which gushes upon his soul as he tastes of the banquet-bowl of heaven. Poetry is the soul of his nature, whereby, from communing with the beauties of this earth, he is capable of giving birth to other beings brighter than himself; and of lifting up his spirit to the presence of those things which he shall enjoy in another state ; and

which he manifests to *this* through the instrument-
ality of certain words and sentences melodiously
concatenated ; and such as correspond with the definite and wise configurations of the mouth in the
communication of thought through language.

There are delineations which grow out of the ca-
pabilities of man, which seem to outshine realities,
but do not, because they spring from the fountains
of things that exist.   There is nothing in the world
that is not equivalent in brightness to the poetical
manifestations of it.   People too often mistake the
relations of things for the *things* themselves.   It is
thus, from the wellsprings of poetry, we draw the
healing fountains of the soul, whereby we baptize
the passions, purify the sentiments, and cause to
spring up in the minds of others the same emotions
that live and breathe in our own.   It is that essence
in the laboratory of the intellect, whereby the soul
transmutes the passions and hallows the sentiments of
man.   It is that divine crucible in which the pas-
sionate ore of the heart is fluxed into the refined gold of moral sentiment.   It is the outpourings
of the skies, and the crystal rivers of the fountain of
Religion.   It is the Pomona of the soul that presides
over the Paradise of the heart.   It is the Caduceus
of all things.

A man who is setting sail for another country—
as all men are—one that is leaving the coral strands
of the sea of life for the great ocean of Eternity—
would feel very poor at the end of his journey, were
he to look back and reflect upon the beautiful shells
he had left behind him upon the shore, and have

no wherewithal at the great day of accounts to pay
his reckoning.

It is therefore gratifying to a man to cull the beautiful flowers from the parterre of life, and feel that
he has held familiar intercourse with the wonderful
things in Nature, and preserved the spotless jewels
of affection in the casket of his heart, as the perqui-
site of days that are to come ; and caught an inspiration from the contemplation of those things, which,
in after life, shall become like Gilead to the soul.

As one that is setting out upon a long journey, and
having nothing better to bequeath the legatees of
his heart, the Author of these poems presents whatever jewels he may have gathered from the regions
of his mind, to their especial care.

The word Nacoochee, in the Indian language,
signifies *beautiful star*. There is a lake, or collection of water, between the Oakmulgee and Flint
rivers, in Georgia, which, during the winter season,
is about three hundred miles in circumference. The
Creek Indians believe that in the centre of this lake
there is an island of such extraordinary beauty, that
if they could only possess it, they would immediately be made happy. They believe that it is inhabit-
ed by the most beautiful of all God's creatures,—
and that they are as lovely as the angels. It is to
them what Elysium was to the ancients, and heaven
to the moderns. It is to them a Fairy-land. They
believe that at some future period they will be in the
possession of that island—which is, to them, the same
as being in Paradise. They believe that the women
are descendants of some great tribe, and some say

that when they approach that Eden of terrestrial bliss, the island continues to move on from them ; so that no one has ever before had the fortune to arrive at that wished-for haven.

They say that there are great chiefs there, who are kings over the immortal rattle-snakes, whose heads are crowned with "*carbuncles*" of such excessive brightness, that they dazzle the island for nine miles around. They say that the great snake, which has this large diamond in his head, leads the rest of the serpents by mowing down the grass before him, by the breath of his nostrils.

They believe that the stones on that island make the most exquisite music, and that the beautiful beings who inhabit it, have the power, like Orpheus, of controlling that music whenever they please.

The musical stones, which are called on the banks of the Oronoco, *Laxas de Musica*, are called *shells* in the poem.

The young man who is called Ostence in the poem, falls in love with one of those celestial beings, whom he tells his father he has seen in a dream. The old man, fired with the enthusiasm of the boy, urges him to build him a boat, and bring the "*Beautiful Star*" to his native land. The old man wishes his son to become great, and tells him how he may be made happy after he is "gathered to his fathers."

The Cherokees believe that if they could possess that beautiful "*carbuncle*" they could immediately buy the whole world. The poem does not stop here, but continues on, and will be published, if proper, at some future day.

The young man, as will be seen from the poem, arrives at that wonderful island, but fearing to approach that *"Beautiful Star,"* remains afar off, while she, alarmed at the sight of so strange a being, prays to Azrael for a deliverance from his contaminating touch, who descends from the clouds in a flood of glory, and bears her away. Thus ends the first Canto.   T. H. C.

New York, Sept. 10*th*, 1837.

CONTENTS.

TO IDEALON.

Soul of the sunny South! thy voice is heard
  In the deep stillness of the virgin heart!
Thy name is coupled with that heavenly word,
  And never from her chambers shall depart!
For thou shalt whisper unto those that sigh
A soothing voice—whose tones shall never die!

Soul of the sunny South! let not thy lays,
  Flung on the waters, perish in the sea!
No! let them come back after many days,
  To feed the heart that once was life to thee!
Go—like the turtle that has left her grove,
And pour thy spirit upon those that love.

NACOOCHEE;

OR,

THE BEAUTIFUL STAR.

I.

BEYOND that wild illimitable waste
Of unfenced prairie, there are wild flowers growing
In rich luxuriance, ever by the chaste
And velvet-vested rivers that are flowing
Within the moss-clad suckle valleys glowing ;
And in that sea-like undulating wild,
The moon-like roses are forever blowing,
For there the wild deer, on the lawn, so mild,
Leaps with the unscared fawn like some delighted child.

II.

And there, amid the suckle-gemmed recesses,
And lawny labyrinthine aisles, afar,
Beyond the green pavilion of the wildernesses,
Bathed in the radiance of the western star,
Like rubies set in emerald—waves the fair
And silken tresses of the spring of vales,
Whose beauty nothing less than heaven can mar !
And *there* the music of the glorious gales
Lift up their voices of long years with heavenly tales.

1

III.

And there, aloft, with his uplifted hand,
The old man stood, with eyes all fire, upon
The margin of that silver lake of sand,
And spoke all loudly to his only son ;
Yes, Ostenee! thy father's race is run !
But listen ! far away upon an isle,
As bright as burnished emerald, there is one
Of the most beautiful !—so like the smile
Of the moon's daughter that she twinkles all the while.

IV.

For *there*, upon that island, soft as even,
The beautiful Nacoochee seems to rise,
All glorious, like the first bright star of heaven,
That burns like sapphire on the azure skies !
And there she has such dark delightful eyes,
The moon's first daughter pales beneath her beams !
And *there* they glimmer with such wild surprise,
That you would liken them to azure streams,
So beautiful are they above our brightest dreams.

V.

And there, upon the southern side, the walls
Of living verdure look like emerald-fire !
For there the music of the waterfalls
Are sweeter than the echoes of the Lyre !
For where the languid blades reach dangling higher,
They cleave the curve-lip shell,—and in the vales
The birds sing sweeter than the heavenly choir,
The song our fathers sang—when, on the gales,
A voice went forth to heaven with man's unearthly wails !

VI.

And there the wild swans of the crystal lake
Woo the enamoured waves, while, softly, there,
The sea-shell crimson through the waters break,
Like first love through the cheeks of beauty fair!
For, underneath her smile, there is no care
To ruffle the bright fountain of thy joy,
But, like that reedy lake, whose dimples are
The young swan's circlings, every thought doth buoy
Her spirits up—whose calmness nothing can destroy.

VII.

Then, Ostenee! thy father bids thee go
To where the green isle, paved with ocean shells,
Looks at the moon upon the waves below—
For *there* the beautiful Nacoochee dwells!
For such, you know, our ancient history tells—
Then, warrior-boy! bright eagle of the race
That bred thy father!—get thee where the spells
Of her fair countenance shall light thy face,
And bear her from that island swiftly to this place.

VIII.

And there that old chief stood upon the sand,
Like copper sculptured into majesty!
For on his dusky brow there sate command,
And on his lips sublime austerity!
And on his cheeks there sate, convulsed, the sea
Of that dark passion of his heart within,
That changed upon his lips tempestuously,
As if his soul were cradled into sin
By those long waving years that made him ghostly thin!

IX.

And in the lofty wildness of the cloud
Of his dark thoughts, there sate immortal gloom!
For now his eyes glared horribly, as proud
As Death while gibbering over Beauty's tomb!
He seemed like some huge fury from the womb
Of Darkness—messenger devout from hell!
Whose spirit seemed upon the world to loom,
For that unslaked revenge which seemed to dwell
In his dark heart—whose secret depths no tongue could tell!

X.

And now the young man bounded from the sand,
And leaping in the boat, he took the oar,
And, standing there awhile, he waved his hand
To that old man who stood upon the shore ;
And sitting down awhile, he left the moor,
And far on through the waters, which he ploughed,
So that the boat was crowned with rainbows, bore
His way, until he came beneath the cloud,
Whereon an angel sat, who spoke to him aloud!

XI.

Behold! upon that spring-clad isle, afar,
Ten thousand footsteps from the solitudes—
A maiden dwells, Nacoochee, the bright star
Of that bright island—Dian of the woods!
And there, around her beauty, naught intrudes,
But the bright dappled fountain of pure shells!
Upon the pavement of whose shore the floods
Break gently, while upon it, nightly, dwells
The daughter of the sun, that half her beauty tells.

XII.

And the beams of her fair countenance fell
On the labyrinthine clouds, like fitful gleams
On Death's dark chariot, on the verge of hell,
Shot from the quiver of those heavenly beams
That light Omnipotence !—and on the streams,
That moan forever in that heavenly vale,
Glanced into glory, like those early dreams
That woo us like the incense on the gale,
Then flit away with that deep joy that made us wail !

XIII.

And then her glorious countenance collected
The still replenished beauty of her smile,
By living upon that which she reflected,
Like the bright lake that dwelt around that isle,
And mirrored back its beauty—all the while
She sate there smiling, from her brightness flowed
A living radiance, streaming round the pile
Of island clouds that in her presence glowed
With that same fulgence which her beauty had bestowed.

XIV.

And there she sate, encircled by the light
Of that deep lustrous lightning, undefiled !
As one that slumbers, dreaming of delight,
As round her snow-white neck the clouds were piled
In floods of ecstacy !—for she was mild—
And through the raven tresses of her hair,
That hung in dalliance on the floatings wild—
Shone the pure brightness of that liquid glare—
But she was unconsumed—her beauty still was fair.

XV.

For the pure whiteness of her swan-like breast
Lay on the background of her raven hair,
All Zephyr-laved, like infancy at rest !
For, on her harp her forehead leaned so fair,
It seemed, beside the strings that glistened there,
Like slanting sunbeams on some mount of snow—
While round her silver sandalled feet the glare
Of the thick lightnings flashed and mantled so,
The liquid quiv'rings burnt with an immortal glow !

XVI.

But far beyond that vision in the sky,
Far on the golden island-clouds that lay
Half buried over ocean, in the dye
Of an immortal azure—*there*, at play,
In the bright regions of eternal day—
An angel fondled with the locks of love !
And on that bright vermilion, far away,
She bore her holy harp, that waved above,
On her fair wings that shone like pinions of the dove.

EXILE OF HEAVEN.

There was upon an isle
    A clear bright river,
And it glittered in the smile
    Of the face of God forever.

And there was upon its green
   An eternal spring for love,
And its river rolled between
   The bright Cherubim above!

And it rolled like molten glass
   To that sapphire silent sea,
Where its waves could never pass
   From that bright eternity.
For they shone like liquid fire,
   In the burning stars of even,
And they rolled not to expire,
   But proceeded out of heaven.

And the waves that circled round
   The eternal mount on high,
Bore an everlasting sound
   To the soul that cannot die.
For the river ran from one
   Of the springs that sparkled in
The bright valley of the sun,
   Where no night hath ever been.

And the crystalline deep sea
   Was cerulean like the even,
When the stars come out to see
   How the soul can get to heaven.
And there was no night, but day
   Was immortal as its beams,
And it could not pass away
   From the spirit of my dreams.

And there was upon its breast
  A great liquid throne of light,
And upon that throne did rest
  A bright Angel drest in white !
And her face was like the skies
  When the heavens are bright above,
And there lived within her eyes
  An eternity of love.

For the deathless mighty flush
  Of her countenance was bright
As the morning, when the gush
  Of her radiance wakes to light.
And her face was as the light
  Of the moon when she is whole,
When she travels in the night
  To the regions of the soul.

And her locks were as the dawn
  Of the morning on the sea,
When the waves are wandering on
  To the borders of the free.
And her language was as deep
  As the earth from heaven above ;
And she sang the moon to sleep
  With an ecstacy of love.

For her brightness seemed to fling
  A deep circlet round the soul,
Like the halo round the ring
  Of the moon when she is whole.

And above her was the glow
   Of a Rainbow beaming bright,
And it spanned the sea below
   With an everlasting light !

And she strode upon the bend
   Of that heaven-exalted bow,
From the sky curve to the end
   Of the firmament below !
For on earth she had been one
   Of the fairest that could be,
And her soul was now the sun
   Of the stars upon the sea.

For Astarte was her name
   In that happy home above ;
But on earth she was the same,
   For her holiness was love.
But away beyond the light
   Of the morning star, was one
Of the brightest of the bright,
   Shining brighter than the sun !

For the souls that entered in
   The bright bosom of the sea,
Are redeemed from mortal sin
   To the joys that are to be ;
When the holy springs are given
   From the fount of life at last,
In the voice that brings from heaven
   An oblivion of the past.

XVII.

And her dark locks lay floating on the breeze,
Like the young lawny verdure of the isles,
Whose wavings are like rollings of the seas,
When from his billows morn reflects her smiles !
And there, all beautiful, like love that wiles
Its leisure, she stood perfect as the day,
When heaven above is cloudless—and the aisles
Of her fair clouds were labyrinthed away,
Like spirits on the blue serene assembled there at play.

XVIII.

And in that tree-shell boat of moderate size,
All lined within with fawn-skins of the woods,
And edged with dappled swan-down, of the dyes
Of the flamingo—fashioned in the solitudes—
And decked with coral where no less intrudes—
The Indian rowed his boat, until he came
To where the sand-beach glittered in the floods,
And there he fastened his small boat, to frame
Some scheme whereby he might approach that heavenly
          dame.

XIX.

And there, all scattered on that island, lay
Ten thousand sea shells, blushing like the hues
Of rich carnation, till the very way
Seemed paved with glory—for the dews
Were all like nectar, and did there diffuse
Such freshness, that from off each damask rim
A musical soft fountain gushed profuse,
So that the air around was one soft hymn
Of eloquence—like that the shells poured forth to him.

XX.

The streams were all like silver—for they seemed,
As by their flowery banks they went their way,
Like heavenly melody, whose gushings gleamed
Like floss unwound by infancy at play,
And tangled on moreen—for, far away
The pearl meanderings glittered in the light,
Till all their windings into that deep bay
Quivered like molten silver!—till the sight
Grew tired with that soft vision which was heavenly bright.

XXI.

And there, upon that island, lay the shells
Of ocean, brimful of the nectar dew,
That dropt from out the golden honey-bells,
And from each rosy sculptured rim of blue,
Leaped with incessant beauty to renew;
And there the languid emerald reeds were seen,
Like lawny plumes, high waving to the view,
On that bright island of immortal green,
Where young Nacoochee stood two heav'nly hills between.

XXII.

And there she stood all beautiful as even,
When the first star begems the cloudless sky,
With eyes as brilliant as the hues of heaven,
When day illumes the firmament on high!
And there, upon that living greensward, by
The crystal rivers—purple as her eyes—
She lifted up her snow-white hands on high,
And pointing to an opening in the skies,
She poured her spirit forth with love that never dies :—

NACOOCHEE'S PRAYER.

ABBA! when my spirit panteth
  For the joys that soon must be;
When the prayers that nature granteth
  Shall be all the world to me;
When the voice that speaks in thunder,
  Shall the universe confound;
When the oaks are rent asunder
  By the lightnings all around;
When the mountains, greatly shaken,
  Shall be buried in the sea,
And my forest home forsaken;
  Lift my spirit up to thee!

Abba! when the reed-isles quiver,
  Where the willow boughs are green,
On the margin of the river,
  Where the Coosa maid is seen;
When the moaning winds are sighing
  Round the cypress in the vale;
When the music-tones are dying
  On the suckle-scented gale;
When the turtle doves are mourning
  In the rose-isles by the sea;
When the stars above are burning,
  Lift my spirit up to thee!

Abba! when the fawns are leaping
  On the lily-bells, that lie
Where the willow-boughs are weeping
  In the stream that trickles by;

When the roe-buck gazes wildly
  At the hunter in the even ;
When the milky moon looks mildly
  From the azure depths of heaven ;
When the hills are clothed in gladness,
  And the valleys laugh with glee ;
When the world is turned to sadness,
  Lift my spirit up to thee !

Abba ! when the big light lingers
  On the fleecy clouds that lie,
As if touched by angels' fingers
  With an everlasting dye ;
When their blond-like edges glisten
  With the golden fringe that shines
Where the angels lean to listen
  To the soul that now repines ;
When the flaky isles of glory
  Sink to slumber on the sea,
And the skies above seem sorry ;
  Lift my spirit up to thee !

Abba ! when the fowls are laving
  In the fountains far away ;
When the purple hills are waving
  To the sunny-isles of day ;
When the mocking-birds are singing
  By the river-banks at noon ;
When the violet-bells are springing
  From the rosy-hills in June ;
When the pigeons all are feeding
  On the beach-mast by the sea ;
When my bosom shall lie bleeding,
  Lift my spirit up to thee !

2

Abba! when the reed is broken,
   That has borne me up when young ;
When the last sad word is spoken,
   That shall tremble on my tongue ;
When the grape-vines all are bending
   O'er the cluster-mirrored stream ;
When the suckle-grove is lending
   Its perfume to every beam ;
When the azure lake is crisping
   By the zephyrs from the sea ;
When no other tongue is lisping,
   Lift my spirit up to thee !

Abba! when the morn is breaking
   Through the portals of the sky ;
When the dappled fawns are waking
   In the reed-isles where they lie ;
When the wanton swan is swimming
   In the zephyr-dimpled lake ;
When her cygnet-down is skimming
   On the waters wide awake ;
When the streams forsake the mountains,
   And return into the sea ;
Abba! save thy little fountains—
   Lift my spirit up to thee !

Abba! when the snow-dove minion
   Takes my forest home at night ;
When the eagle breaks his pinion
   In the swiftness of his flight ;
When the roe-buck comes to wander
   From the green hills far away ;
When my beating heart grows fonder
   For the sunny isles of day ;

When my forest home is taken,
    And the stranger bids me flee ;
Abba ! call me thy forsaken—
    Take my *spirit* home to thee !

XXIII.

And she stood there alone, addressing heaven,
In holy attitude—what did she see ?
An angel fondling with the locks of even,
In holy vestments, coming from the sea
Of righteousness beyond eternity !
And she was crowned with stars that never set,
As round her feet ran rivers joyfully,
Beneath the holy cherubim, that met
Beside the mercy-seat, where angels worship yet.

XXIV.

And then his soul was troubled like the lake
Beside the tasselled reed-isle, where the fawn,
All beautiful, beneath the blades, awake,
Doth watch the eddyings of the milky swan
Upon the placid waters, circling on ;
As from her breast forever doth arise
The music of her billows, which, upon
The shore breaks into language, like the sighs
Of his soft breast, whose heavings burst forth in his eyes.

XXV.

And long upon his spirit did she break
The crystal clearness of that holy sea !
And like the milky swan upon the lake,
Broke up the waves of his dark memory
To rapture tones, which spread incessantly
Upon the chambers of his heart, and wore
A caverned labyrinth, which grew to be
A place most mournful—till his heart's deep core
Sank into that deep sea whose ripples had no shore !

XXVI.

For in that island of ten thousand dyes,
Beside the liquid gushings of the springs
That waved beneath the azure of her eyes,
She made her fingers tremble on the strings
With an immortal music !—till the wings
Of twice ten thousand angels seemed around
The wooings of her harp, like artless things,
And, while they bathed them in the waves of sound,
They crowned her with the flowers with which her harp
      was bound.

XXVII.

And the seductive foldings of her dress,
Of sky-blue satin, waved around her form
Beneath, in rich voluptuous gentleness,
As through those foldings beat her heart, as warm
As that deep glow upon her cheeks, whose charm
Told eloquently what lay couched beneath ;
As on her ruby-cinctured lips alarm
Sat throned, while, from the sweetness of her breath,
A melody gushed forth, like eloquence in death !

XXVIII.

And in the richness of that flowery grove
Of golden oranges, she lived alone ;
So that she seemed like Psyche crowned by Love,
Save when the angels tendered her their own ;
And when the ravished sweetness of the tone
Of their soul's language settled in her heart,
It seemed but as an impulse of her own ;
And with the utterings of her lips apart,
She caused the wind-waked silence into song to start !

XXIX.

Her eyes were very lustrous, and so large
They looked like darkness baptized in the light
Of an immortal glory—like some barge,
All newly built, beneath the moon at night,
And rocking on the waters !—they were bright
As an immortal glory set in heaven !
When all around its radiance is delight,
And that delight her smiles !—as fair as even
When from the sunlit skies the very clouds are driven.

XXX.

Her voice was like Religion's, and the tone
Was mellow, like the flute-strains on the hills
At midnight, heard but by the loved alone,
When stars are fondling with the mountain rills—
For she was that divinity which fills
The poet's spirit when he dreams of heaven,
And gives his inspiration that which kills
All sorrow,—when his thoughts go forth at even
To worship God beneath the light that he has given.

2 2

XXXI.

Oh ! had you wandered from his copse along
The lily-banks that looked upon the stream,
In dewy softness, listening to the song
She sung herself beneath bright Cynthia's beam,
That sprinkled round her loveliness the gleam
Of radiant glory—shed among the flowers—
And those dark locks that made her blushes teem
With lively fulgence—love's immortal powers—
Oh ! you had thought Nacoochee queen of all the Hours.

XXXII.

Oh! had you seen her thus beneath the moon,
Her snow-white bosom heaving like the sea !
As some tall mountain spread with snow at noon,
Her dark, long locks all sweeping lavishly—
As each soft breeze came fondling them for me !
Her dark bright eyes upturned upon the sky,
With two pearl tear-drops fringing them, to be
A living truth that she was born to die !—
Oh ! had you seen her thus, how deep had been the sigh!

XXXIII.

He looked upon her features with delight—
A chiselled masterpiece almost divine—
The artist, God !—She lay along the light
Of Luna, streaming round her form supine,
And striving on her loveliness to shine,
Whose mellow radiance gave unto her eyes
A languid glory—till she seemed to pine
In her own radiance—mingling her surprise
With that soft innocence which she could not disguise.

XXXIV.

There gushed upon her cheeks, beneath her eyes,
A vigilant sublimity, that seemed
To those, who gazed upon her with surprise,
As if they had, despairingly, but dreamed
Of some Utopian loveliness, they deemed
Of some celestial sphere, which God had given
To make creation heaven!—Around her beamed
A living rainbow, softer than the even,
With two bright, missioned seraphs watching her from
    heaven!

XXXV.

Her facial *contour* gave unto her smiles
A modelled tenderness, that seemed to melt
In their own mellowness, like distant isles
In ocean—while, upon her features dwelt
A virgin pleasantness, most often felt
In ideal poetry—whose blushes shone
Like sunlit skies when Autumn is the belt
That girds creation—while, beneath her zone,
A passion dwelt, almost unto herself unknown.

XXXVI.

And when she spoke, her words, upon her tongue,
Were jewels, that reluctant seemed to fall,
As soft celestial nectar round them clung,
That turned her lisping accents, gently small,
To angel eloquence—that gave to all
A mellifluent cadence, turned to love
And harmony!—Upon her lips no gall
Was ever known—but, like unto the dove,
The words she spoke were truths that came from heaven
    above.

XXXVII.

Her deep-dyed lips were crimson with the blood
Of healthy newness—making each fond smile
That waltzed upon her lips, flush with the flood
Of nectar softness, making love turn exile
In despair—although, alas! she might awhile
Make earth celestial, then return to be
The thing she was before she made this isle
A new Elysium—who was unto me,
A fountain, when most thirsty, deeper than the sea.

XXXVIII.

An untold indescribable delight
Of modesty collected round her form—
An angel majesty, that gave me light
To contemplate her through the storm
Of my soul's rapture, raging now to warm
Me into poetry—impress my heart
With that she was in heaven,—blest—uniform—
A paradise imbodied without art—
As sunshine upon snow-drops dazzling every part.

XXXIX.

Behind yon everlasting pensile pall,
That hangs above creation, from the frown
Of thunder-gusts that into ocean fall—
Behold! th' impending torrents gushing down!
Lo! lightnings flashing every cloud to crown !
Whose avalanche-like roar now shakes the plains!
As clouds torn flying after others flown,
The only trophy left for all their pains,
The thirsty earth lies drenched with cloud-devouring
    rains.

XL.

The oaks leviathan, shattered by the nod
Of these almighty elements, fall down
In dread abasement, howling out to God
And Nature, whose omnipotent renown
Transcends eternity—beneath whose frown
Of dreadful majesty He rules the stars
That light immensity—upon whose crown
They shine above earth's elemental wars—
And whose right hand breaks down even hell's infernal
    bars!

XLI.

And now aloft, above this howling vast,
The heart's blood curdling into frightful fear!
A soaring Angel sails above the blast,
And leaves another following in the rear!
Nor turns she back upon destruction near,
But, tempest towering, rises to the sky,
On heaven's eternal verge, where all is clear,
As one tremendous peal comes rolling nigh,
And shakes her soul again, entranced—earth-bound—to
    die!

XLII.

And now yon dark tremendous battlement
Of exiled clouds, dispersing seaward o'er,
Through heaven's eternal battle-fields unspent,
Leaves God's high canopy baptized once more!
On whose cerulean plains ofttimes before,
This Armageddon battle has been fought;
As now comes ardent sunshine down to pour
A new-born vigour into frightened thought,
And earth again seems pregnant with new glory fraught.

XLIII.

And over every stormy terror bound,
A sweet refreshment circles every thing;
And over earth's deep stillness comes, profound,
A settling silence, sleeping on the wing
Of brooding zephyrs, while above doth spring,
From God's high brazen canopy divine,
A gushing radiance, till the birds do sing,
And heaven's complacent countenance doth shine,
And earth exults that each fierce bolt remains supine.

XLIV.

The tottering clouds now reel along the light
Of lustrous lightnings, as they vanish on,
And earth seems mellowed into sad delight,
As dying thunder echoes—it is gone!
An awful silence reigns on earth alone !
The overflowing rivers rush along,
In lordly grandeur, gurgling to the tone
Of lowland chorister, whose wakeful song
Is more than gladly heard these languid flowers among.

XLV.

But lo ! from out the reedy isles that lay
Far over ocean, northward of that lake,
A charger wonderful did make his way,
And the smooth surface of the waters break !
For he was beautiful as clouds that flake
The dim horizon—fawn-like was his skin—
Of multi-coloured mail—whose speed did make
An iris-coloured foam before his thin
And dusky keel, which pleased the waves he wandered in.

XLVI.

And from his nostrils, lifted high in air,
An incense-cloud ascended, like the smoke
From off an altar, when perfume is there,
And round the forelocks of that charger broke
With such bright wreathings, that the vision woke
The idea of Divinity arrayed in light ;
Which clung around that rider as he spoke,
Like an immortal whirlwind in the night,
Winged by the burning tempest with volcanic might !

XLVII.

Bathed in the glory of ten thousand clouds,
The snow-white charger galloped on the storm !
And mantled with the brightest of all shrouds,
Rushed in his glory to that heavenly form !
But seeing that his brightness might alarm
The softest of all beings where she stood—
Mantled his face with an immortal charm,
And gathering round her beauty with the flood
Of his bright beams, filled her with an immortal good !

XLVIII.

And on that whirlwind of immortal fire,
The charger galloped with eternal light !
And pawing with the thunders of his ire,
Shone like the lightnings of the clouds at night,
Upon the wings of Darkness ! Oh ! that sight !
And, rushing onward, dashed to that frail form !
And, yielding to his rider, checked his flight,
And snorting like the thunders of the storm—
Bore her away amid the shouts of her alarm !

XLIX.

And upward—far beyond the things of time—
He rose, rejoicing that his arm was strong !
And rising into that high home sublime,
Poured forth his voice with an immortal song !
Which, soaring into heaven, the stars among,
Filled up the universe, as on it went,
With melody—gave heaven another tongue—
And unto all the spheres an echo lent,
And, rolling—died like glory upon the firmament.

L.

Thank God for thy deliverance, blessed child !
Thank God for thy redemption ! There was pain
In that dark region round the eternal wild,
Where thou shalt never more be seen again !
And he shall look upon that isle in vain !
The waterfalls shall never more to thee
Give back the echo of thy voice, like rain !
And never shall thy form divide the sea,
Where sleeps the silver moon—Oh, no ! for thou art free !

LI.

And there were seraphs crying in the spheres,
As they were passing onward to the blest ;
And from each other's eyes were shed the tears
That fell from heaven for Palestine's behest !
And there were voices crying in the west,
And saying, Wake, Nacoochee !—loved ! awake !
And put thy garments on—prepare thy rest—
For thou shalt die !—thy time is come !—partake
Of this thy marriage supper—ready for thy sake !

LII.

And thus enveloped in that mighty flood
Of everlasting glory, rushed the steed
To her deliverance!—There she stood!
And who shall recompense that rider for the deed?
And where was Ostence?—borne like the reed
That meets the torrent's course—he fell like stone!
But thou, Nacoochee! loved one! thou wert freed
From this world's sorrow!—thou art now alone
In that bright region round th' Eternal's heavenly throne!

LIII.

She wept for joy!   His soul was on the gales
Of morning, answering back again to even—
When lo! another voice, from out the vales,
Said, *See yon Rainbow coming down from heaven!*
He looked!   Behold! Nacoochee! with the seven
That loved her!—Angels—Cherubs—all, divine!
In spiritual glory passed above him, given—
God—God! thou didst redeem unto him, thine!
And saved his precious jewel with thyself to shine!

LIV.

And she was changed among terrestrial things—
She died!—Her soul was borne above the spheres
In joy triumphant!—borne upon the wings
Of angels unto God's high home, where tears
Nor sorrow dwell!—where there are no deep cares—
And no rejoicings but of pure delight!
A parting felt when life had fewer years—
When there was unto him no day, but night,
And that dark pall which hangs upon his spirit's light!

LV.

Ah! who can feel intoxicating love,
The sweetest boon that recollection brings—
And not inhale perfumes from heaven above,
And drink delight from hope's celestial wings?
The last drop that existence faintly flings
From Memory's cup, tastes sweeter than the first—
The bottom gathers sweetness from the springs
Of life, when other feelings we have nursed
Are gone—when life no more for earthly things shall thirst!

LVI.

And now his lonely spirit would be gone,
But cannot go—still yearning for the sky!
For longing only makes him more alone,
In this dark world—where love can never die!
The birds have their appointed times to hie—
The foxes, too, have holes—then let him rest
In hopes that when his God shall pass him by,
His hand will lead his spirit to the rest
Of his Nacoochee, where her soul is haply blest.

LVII.

Oh, God! that thou hadst made him something more
Than this sad thing—this broken-hearted wight!
A barren tree upon life's sandy shore,
That never more shall flourish with delight!
The sunshine has departed from his sight!
The dearest thing that ever was to be!
Yon reedy-isle now hides her from his sight—
Oh! that his wounded spirit could be free,
To lay his broken heart, Nacoochee, down with thee!

LVIII.

Earth had no sweeter thing than that bright one—
That heaven-exalted child! for she was fair
As isles that gem the ocean!—she is gone
To that bright world where there is no despair!
And she shall bind the roses in her hair
No more in this dark world!—nor deck her brow!
And she shall never more attune the air
To that sweet music, which was as the vow
Of an immortal—Lord! where is that beauty now?

LIX.

She is not in this world—she is afar!
In that bright region where the angels dwell!
And when we gaze upon yon western star,
We think that we can hear that herald tell
Of that bright being, who, from out the well
Of this world's wilderness, drank but the dew
Of heaven descending!—fitting her too well
For that immortal rest—as if she knew
Her time was come when she should bid this world adieu!

LX.

And now we gaze upon the vales—the brooks—
And on the mountains where that blessed stood!
And on the valleys, where the owlet nooks
Threw shadows on the twilight of the wood,
And we may gaze upon that glorious flood,
And pluck the flowers that she has gazed upon;
And touch the boughs that made her solitude—
But never more, beneath yon heavenly sun,
Shall we behold that being—that immortal one!

LXI.

And we shall see that lovely one to-morrow—
Oh! never more! that gentle one no more!
And we shall feel for her immortal sorrow,
And plunge despair into our heart's deep core!
To weigh the love that caused our hearts to pour
Its grief out over her with such despair,
Must make them both immortal!—Life is o'er!
And we must learn from ills what is to bear
A love so mournful—till our spirits turn to prayer!

LXII.

And that immortal island—*that* shall never,
In all this world, behold her beauty more!
For that which was shall there remain forever!
And spring may come upon that sunny shore,
And flowers may spring up like the flowers of yore;
And birds may sing the sweetness of the even,
And hearts may break as they have broke before;
And time may mend the chords that he has riven—
But *never*, through all time, shall she return from heaven!

LXIII.

Thou lonely star! that first born of the even,
In yonder high blue world, beholds me here—
I gaze upon thee, until all in heaven
Seems borne upon me from thy distant sphere!
I see thee shine no larger than the tear
That now thy beauty likens in mine eyes—
A pearl-drop, pensile from thine own parterre,
That liftest my spirit with devout surprise
To claim my cherished home beyond thy deep blue skies,

LXIV.

Thou precious realm! that, pensile to the world,
Now keep'st me yearning for my home above—
An earth-bound spirit, whose bright wings are furled
To know that thou art happy with my love!
I would that thou couldst meet me with the dove
The dear bright thing that never shall return
To make me happy—for my thoughts must rove,
And my lamentings nurture me to mourn
For that bright hour when she was from my presence
    torn!

LXV.

And art thou, little star! unto the blest,
A bright Elysium, like thy light to me?
And dost thou yield unto Nacoochee's rest,
The glorious joy that she demands of thee?
Oh, thou! that settest thy face upon the sea,
And comest from thy far home upon the streams—
That teachest my spirit what it is to be
In heaven—art thou, with all thy silver beams,
To pass off gently like my first love's early dreams?

XLVI.

And art thou habited with brighter things
Than earth?—thou look'st upon me from afar!
And have thy mountains many sweeter springs
Than these, where thou art my Nacoochee's star?
And have thine angels brighter hopes, to mar
The circumventings that await the soul?
And does thy sapphire glimpse attend the car
That bearest my dear Nacoochee to the goal
Of God, where she shall all these many pangs console?
  3 3

LXVII.

And now, with my devotion, let me raise
My gentle harp-strings unto Thee, the wise
And great Jehovah!—who art worth all praise—
The deep exhaustless worship of the skies!
The glorious hallelujah's that arise,
And answer back rejoicing to the spheres,
In that deep angel-burst that never dies!
Whose melodies shall wipe away all tears
From human eyes, great God! through thine eternal
        years!

LXVIII.

Then, gentle harp! awake no more to die!
The soft sweet tones that made thee as the dove
In summer—leave me here alone to sigh!
'Tis silence! thou shalt answer me above!
But who, alas! shall bear me to the love
Of my Nacoochee!—she, who was to me,
As bird-songs unto silence, when the grove
Is listening to the music anxiously—
As shell-tones unto isles that dwell upon the sea.

LXIX.

Thou hast been unto me, my gentle one!
A minister, whose melodies were love!
A comforter, amid my griefs, when none
Could reconcile me—save that one above!
And now, my blessed being! like the dove
That wails her mate, my spirit turns to thee!
While on the silver willow in the grove
I hang my harp—Æolia! play for me
A farewell song, when this sad life shall cease to be!

LXX.

As thou hast been unto me as the food
A mother yields her children from her breast—
The careful dove that wings her little brood,
And sets them safe beneath her own to rest ;
As thou hast come unto me, from the blest
In heaven, amid descending dews at night,
And wrestled with my spirit in the west,
In voiceless silence—when there was no light
But thine—thou holiest seraph of the best
In heaven!—my spirit turns again to thy behest!

LXXI.

For thou shalt feed upon the fire of heaven
In wasteless glory—thou shalt reap the lore
Of life forever—blest—redeemed—forgiven !
And thou shalt reign forever on the shore
Of Christ immortal—changeless ever more !
And thou shalt sail upon that glorious sea,
Where no dark waves shall ever sweep it o'er—
For thine eternal heritage shall be
A deep, bright, rosy morn—forever noon to thee.

THE DEATH OF TIME.

And every island fled away, and the mountains were not found.

Rev. 16 : 20.

LISTEN! what mysterious sounds are those
That roll through heaven?—what melodious songs!
And why that glorious song of ocean, where
The heavens are mirrored back upon his waste?
It is the mighty minstrelsy of storms
Borne on the rustlings of an angel's wings!
And what is that bright image in the sun?
An angel fondling with the locks of Christ!
For, lo! from out the confines of the sky,
A Tragedy of most celestial light,
Whose Acts were written by the hands of God,
And whose eventful scenes were laid in heaven,
And where the Dramatist, that now appears
In the last Act, was born—bursts forth in floods
Of glory on the soul! For now it seems
As if the words were syllabled in stars
Of living light, bathed in the hues of heaven!
For in the fifth Act, when the Lord of life
And glory shall appear, arrayed in robes
Of righteousness, with one foot on the neck
Of Death, the other on the mouth of hell,
And drawn by steeds of lightning down the aisles
Of constellated glory—there shall come
Ten thousand whirlwinds from the sea of God!
And with the mighty eloquence of winds,

That sweep the wild illimitable waste
Of unfenced prairie, where the exiled tones
Of ocean gather up in prayer to God;
And where the grisly darkness of the woods
Sends out the tempests to the azure hills,
And from the frowning solitudes are torn
The sinuous tendons of the giant oaks—
Shall join the hallelujah of the storms,
And hail, with one celestial waft of joy,
The embrace of the nations! And the caves
Of mighty mountains, whose sky-cleaving heads
Are crowned with everlasting snows, shall wave
Their land-tones over ocean, like the shell,
Whose deep celestial melody shall fly
To meet the organ of Eternity,
And roll the waves of thunder into heaven!
And now the Lord of glory raised on high,
With right hand lifted half way into heaven—
Grasping twice ten thousand thunders in his fists,
And sounding like the crush of falling worlds—
Commands the sun to stop his course and die!
Time is appalled! the moon is struck with fear!
And palsy rains decrepitude on earth!
For, faithful to his summons, he prepares,
With all his rich magnificence of stars,
And with his glorious pageantry of spheres,
To see the mighty martyrdom of Death!
And at the funeral of the corpse of Time,
Behold the angels dig his grave in chaos!
And now from out his lifted hand on high,
Down—down—the seven-bolted thunder falls!
And from the adamantine gates of hell
Tears the rude bars asunder—while, anon,
The Devil, from his confines, drags from out

The fiery fingers of the fiends of hell
The clanking chains of vengeance, newly forged,
And on the rusty heels that trod the graves
Of empires, sets the everlasting seal
Of Destiny that never shall be loosed!
And now the mighty organ of the sea
Takes up the requiem of the falling stars!
A mournful anthem comes from out the moon!
For she has found her grave-clothes in the clouds !
And frightened at the widowhood of earth,
She wanders blindfold from her wonted path,
And, wailing for her ocean-lord, she puts
On sackcloth for the dying sun, and sets
Behind Eternity to rise no more!
And now, with mandates louder than the shout
Of congregated Angels when they sang
The advent of the dawn of Time, and tolled
The requiem of his demise on the stars—
The voice of Christ goes forth among the dead,
With tidings that shall be remembered when
Eternity shall be no more—ARISE !
And quick to live as was the sun to die,
The buried nations of the universe
Threw off the dusted winding sheet of death,
And from the sepulchre that coffins Time,
Stood up erect in attitude divine,
And saw the radiance of the smiles of God!
And now old ocean, frozen at the voice
That shook effulgence from the sun, yields up
The dead that lay within him—for his waves
Were crystalled into darkness by the night
That wrapped the universe in gloom, and wove
The murky shroud that sepulchred the sun—
And breathless as the silence that lay couched

Upon his bosom, tombes the songless spheres!
For down into that everlasting sea,
Ten thousand, thousand fathoms deep, they sank
Beneath the thunders of Messiah's voice!
And those that slept within the coral caves,
And braved the pantings of that mighty sea;
And those that slept upon his briny couch,
And folded in the drapery of his waves;
And those long cradled on his locks of age,
That dreamed amid the shell-tones of that Day—
Arose in lineaments divine, and heard
The glorious shoutings of the host of God!
And far beyond that sea—behind the hills
Of darkness—where the sun had gone to rest—
And where the confines of primeval night
Gave forth creation—where the grave of Time
Was dug by Angels—*there* the heavens were seen!
And now redeemed from mortal death to life!
And from the wages of that dreamless sleep!
And from the bony embrace of the dead!
And roused from out the Dædal couch of clay,
By that delightful summons—they go forth!
And robed in that excessive light which tore
The veil of hell's impenetrable gloom,
To scan the hills of Immortality—
And from the shackles of perpetual night,
Throned on the highest hills of God—they see
The shoreless ocean of Eternity!
And from the lawny isles that skirt the waves
Of vale-meandering streams that gush along
In pleasant journeyings to the sea of life—
They pluck the luscious clusters—and from groves
That float on frankincense, they take their harps—
And on the greensward by the hills of heaven,

That look upon the Sharon of the Lamb—
They gather up an ocean of sweet sound ;
And while they strike the interludes of joy,
Fill up the embrace of perpetual love.
But never, while Eternity shall roll
To mock the grandeur of creation, shall
The thunders of dissolving Nature preach
The funeral of the death of Time—nor hail
Again the resurrection of the just.

THE SOARING SWAN,

SEEN FROM THE ALLEGANY MOUNTAINS.

Thou art soaring away, beautiful bird !
Upon thy pinions into distant lands—
Bathing thy downy bosom's loftiest flight
In welkin zephyrs !—Whither art thou borne
From snowy home through heaven's empyrean depths ?
That seem'st, above my soul's uplifted gaze,
A snow-fleece newly shorn from Shiloh's lambs,
And drop half way from heaven !—Thou art alone,
In pearl-tinct azure, pathless, bent for rest,
As now thy pillowed wings are cleaving heaven !
A turtle-dove transition may thy soul
Enjoy while passing into paradise.
Thou'rt buried, artless emigrant, in heaven !
Thou digg'st thy grave among exalted clouds !
God bless thy joyful flight ! may seraphs guide
Thy lonely passport unto sun-sought climes,

And woo thy way above unvarying earth.
Fly on, sweet bird ! thy voice alone can soothe
Thy clamorous mate, whose tones are all the strains
That language eloquent can well impart—
Go ! wind thy wanton neck around her own,
As lovers' arms entwined—with bitter tears—
And recompense her undiminished love !
Oh ! listen gently to her clarion voice !
It drops like waves of glory to the earth !
While in the welkin of the skies, the clouds,
Like undulating isles spread out upon
The ocean of eternity, appear
In lawny prospect, like the sweets of some
Ambrosial grove whose incense waves to heaven.
And far away they gather into floods
Of glory, like the waves of sound that came
From Ocean, when the wings of angels flew
To Salem with the music of the Lord.
For now they waltz upon the fields of space,
Wrapped in the glorious embrace of the sun,
In concert with the music of the spheres.
Fly on, celestial bird ! for thou shalt rest
Upon the waters of that sunny land
To which thou goest, when, upon thy wings,
Bathed in the fleecy bankments of the sky,
No angels lean to listen to the soul
That now repines !—Go ! mingle with thine own,
And they shall be like Gilead to the soul !
For like the healing wells of old, when on
The soul fell Siloah's waters—when from heaven
The rivers of salvation flowed to heal
The nations—shall around thy bosom flow
The crystal fountains ! For, beneath thy voice
A ripple shall go forth, so heavenly sweet,

That it shall be, around thy reedy isles,
Like Judah's harp that on the willow boughs
Hung over Jordan. There, the dove shall sigh!
And in that sunny land where all is peace—
Though constancy is thine—thy soul shall learn
A precept from her—*seek no second love!*
But if thy silver mate should die, sail on
To some transporting scene, where, on the streams,
Beside the tasselled reed-isles, thou shalt hear
The mellow cadence of the winds, and soothe
Thy weary soul once more. For there shall flow
From out the circlings of thy floating form,
Bathed in the flickering dalliance of the gems
Of thy sun-cinctured dimples, like the pearl
Of ocean set in beryl by the deep—
A shell-toned music—whose deep sound shall be
As soft as that sweet sigh of angels, when
They whisper to the soul celestial peace.

Thou art soaring around the throne of light,
Bathed in the tingling radiance of the sun,
Whose bright effulgence, gilding thine abyss
Of burnished glory, scales the heights of heaven!
For on the velvet vesture of the hills,
Throned in the fulgence of celestial day,
In desert embrace—bosomed by the groves—
And where the liquid flowings of the waves
Woo the enamoured banks—thy home shall be.
And from the silver woof of osier boughs,
Bathed in the balmy tears of dewy night,
The spirits of the universe shall weave
A green pavilion for thy winter couch,
And cause the mantle of thy languid mail
To dabble in the ripples of the stream.

And there the long pent music of the voice
Of Nature shall go forth among the aisles,
And shake from off the beaded suckle-boughs,
The nectar dews, whose rustlings on the streams
Shall wake new waves of melody to rise
From out the lily dimples, like the sighs
Of beauty fondling with the locks of love.
For they shall fall as soft upon that lake,
As if an angel's hand had stricken them
From out the leaning rainbows, which were made
A rainbow-harp, whose seven strings were hues.
And there upon the halcyon of thy home,
Bathed in the radiant glimmerings of thy waves—
Burning like molten silver—thou shalt rest—
And with the gushings of thy silver voice,
Fill up the embrace of thy dimples, till,
Upon the waves of thy soft circlings, there
Shall ride the coursing tones of joy, and melt
In kisses on the dewy-mantled shore.
And from the labyrinthine aisles of flowers,
Upon the suckle-scented gales, shall flow
The rich balsamic odours of the spring,
And from the bare arms of the boughs, shall rain
The luscious clusters, till their tones shall be
As soft as the first audible steps of one
Beloved, at the last meeting, heard at night.
And when the curtains of dark night shall fall
Upon the eyelids of the day, and leave the locks
Of darkness sprinkled with the stars ; and when
From out the folds of Night shall steal the moon
To bathe in thy sweet waters—take thy rest—
Then couch thy silver head beneath thy wing,
And as the breeze would bear thee, float, and learn
To reconcile thy sorrows with the winds.

Thou'rt gone, celestial bird!—thy pinions fade!
I linger here, gazing upon thy lessening form,
Buoyant between two distant worlds, outspread—
Like lovers parting—those who meet no more!
As night, dark night! her mantle gathers round,
Wrapping thy milky form with dusky shroud.

Oh! when prepared from this reluctant world—
Wishing thy journey mine—wishing in vain—
To pass my solitude—may thine own wings
Await my spirit home—exalted—blest!
And while alone my longing spirit soars—
Yearning that thou art lost—that thou art gone—
The soul that thou dost leave this day, shall live,
And live forever—shine with heavenly light—
Mourning that thou art happier still than man—
And like thy side-long pinions enter heaven.

THE LAST WRECK.

THERE was deep silence in the heaven of heavens!
For all the herbs were withered on the earth,
And there was nothing perishable left,
But the abodes of men, all, tenantless!
For they had passed away into the dim
And silent house appointed for the dead!
And far, like sheetless ghosts that stalked the world,
The skeleton of giant oaks stood up,
As if to mock the attitudes of men,
And in the lurid flickerings of the sun,

That sent his dying glare athwart the heavens,
Pierced the dim thickness of that mortal night!
For the far-stretching solitudes were torn
By the tempestuous whirlwinds, as they came
From out the nostrils of the dying sea!
And when the pantings of his collapsed sides
Gave out the last Lunarian sigh to heaven,
That sent prolific torpor through his limbs;
And when the voiceless confines of his waves
Lay back within the pulseless arms of his
Peninsulas, with one far-spreading seethe
Of songless palsy—down his bosom sank!
And when the sighs of his last burthen broke
Upon the ear of that dim silence—loud
As an immortal thunder—all was done!
And those far-waving locks that had been combed
Back from the shore by the tempestuous winds,
Lay scattered into silent loneliness!
And where the dusted bones of Empires lay
In wild confusion—that were made the brick
And mortar for the palaces of kings—
And where the souls of men were borne upon
The wings of genius into glory—where
The mildewed chains of infamy were linked
And riveted around the hearts of old—
No music-laden surge came forth to lave
The mighty mistress of that frozen sea!
But far off from that antiquated fane,
Embayed in the dim regions of thick ice,
A lonely ship lay bosomed in the sea!
For she had been the mightiest of the deep—
But now she stood alone, all motionless,
A jewel set in darkness!—for her masts
Were torn asunder by the winds—and there,

4 4

Half buried in the freezings of the deep,
That fell beside the foldings of her sails—
The fractured ends stood piercing the dim night!
And there, in painful quietude, she sate,
As if she listened for soundless sea,
And heard the far off comings of the winds!
But there was never more, beyond the realms
Of that eternal night, another day,
In whose bright regions she might float in joy!
But there, upon the night-time of that deck,
A maiden, beautiful above all things,
As perfect as the very day she died—
Lay prostrate, with her clenched hands on her breast!
For on the brightness of her curling lips
Sate scornfully the triumph of the heart
That in her lifetime made her beautiful!
And from her eyelids hung, congealed, the tears
That she had shed in her despair—and *there*,
To keep the good ship company, she lay,
Grasping the dagger that had done the deed!
And by her side the bones of him who would
Have robbed her of her honour—for she drew
The bloody weapon, which she grappled still,
And plunged it in her heart—and so she died!
And there his ashes lay upon the deck,
As if they had been moistened by the tears
Of angels, as they bore away her soul—
All trodden into powder by the feet
Of hell's infernal legionry, when sent
To drag his spirit into endless death!
And in the sunless silence of that night,
As if she waited for the angels, slept
The beautiful in death, to show the world
That VIRTUE shall survive the wreck of Time.

HOLY LOVE.

"That light whose smile kindles the universe."

Adonais.

THERE is joy in such love beyond all that is known,
When it comes like the first song that infancy hears,
When its young heart receives, for the first time, the tone
That it gives back again with an echo of tears.
For the miner that takes from the cold earth the stone
That he wears on his breast as it came from the sod,
Is too poor for the purchase of love only known
        Unto God, unto God.

As the Indian that leaves in the pride of his chase
Every footprint that turns in the mire to stone,
That shall last when the type shall depart from the place,
And the children that knew him forever unknown ;
As the nations may pass from the green earth away,
Though the footprints shall wear deeper still in the sod—
So the soul undefiled shall ascend on its way
        Unto God, unto God.

It is love like the music that comes from the stream,
When the waves are the tones that the shoals make
        beneath,
If the heart meet with clouds, when the sunshine shall
        gleam,

Then the love that it yields will be stronger than death!
There is joy in such love beyond all that is known,
When the soul in its purity makes its abode
In the heart that it loves, while it yields up its own
        Unto God, unto God.

It is love like the moan, when the winter is nigh,
Of the cavern whose dungeon no mortal can know,
Till the tempest shall come on its cold lips to sigh,
And the mouth of its chaos breathe accents of wo!
It is thus with the heart when it sighs all alone
For the loved one that filled up its sunless abode,
For the loss of that love it must give out its own
        Unto God, unto God.

It is love undefiled, that, from selfishness, seeks
A new language its own ocean depths to express,
And will covet each thought that it wilfully speaks,
Though, if lavished by others, were useless excess.
It is love that forgets every love but its own,
And, in loving, would seek some diviner abode,
Where its fulness, by rising, might flow on alone
        Unto God, unto God.

It is love that can live in the cold breath of scorn,
If the loved one will only be gay with the gay—
For the cloud that shall come on the light of its morn,
Is the one that reflects but the heaven of day.
It is love that will pant like the hart for the brook,
When pursued by the hounds from its native abode,
And though driven afar on the cold world, will look
        Unto God, unto God.

It is love that can dwell in the cool shady bower,
Where the loved one was seen in the days of his youth ;
And commune with delight on the thoughts of that hour,
When the lips of his soul spoke the music of truth.
It is love that can weep at the sound of the tone
Like the one that was heard when the heart overflowed,
When the prayers that were offered were lifted alone
                Unto God, unto God.

If the turtle should wander away from her nest,
She may come back again from the isles of the sea ;
If the swan should depart from her cold world to rest
In some other bright land where her fellows may be—
She may come back again—but the spirit once flown,
It shall never return to its former abode !
But shall rest, like the Pleiade that wanders alone,
                With its God, with its God.

THE DYING POET.

"Truly my soul waiteth upon God ; from him cometh my salvation."
                                        Psalms, 62 : 1.

WITHIN my heart there seems to burn
    A fire that soon must cease !
To make my wandering soul return
    To that bright world of peace !
A little while this storm shall rage,
    And then 'twill all be o'er !
The cold wan light shall then engage
    My burning heart no more !

Within my heart there seems to beat
  A pulse that soon must be
The precious food for worms to eat
  Of wasting energy!
The fiery soul that fed on love,
  From this worn frame must part!
And there, forever, like the dove,
  Be mateless from the heart!

The dismal, shadowy vale that lies
  In death's dark region there,
Is now between my tearful eyes
  And heaven—where all is fair!
The place where there is neither pain
  Nor wo would be the spot
Where this lone frame would rest in vain,
  If there its home were not.

I would not lay my body down
  On this lone dreamless bed,
Were there no trophies in the crown
  We wear beyond the dead!
And what were this cold mockery here?
  If there were not away,
The glorious blessings of the year
  Of God's eternal day!

The deep, dark chaos of the night
  That has no morrow near!
The cold, sad yearnings for the light
  That never shall appear!
Oh! ask me not if this can be—
  The stars would all be riven!
And *thunders*, from eternity,
  Would silence all in heaven!

I feel these aspirations are
  But tokens from above,
To lift my parting spirit near
  The paradigms of love!
The pensive star that reigns on high,
  Lives also on the deep;
And thus my soul shall cleave the sky,
  While here my heart must sleep!

The young year's youngest flowers that grew,
  And garlanded my brow,
Are slain beneath the heavy dew,
  And all are withered now!
The stricken heart that feels no more
  The pain that once it felt,
Has, from its deepest chambers, tore
  The tears that made it melt!

I need not linger here to free
  The soul that cannot fill!
For though my food were as the sea,
  My heart would hunger still!
I see that earth cannot suffice
  To give my spirit rest;
I now will feed upon the skies,
  And sing among the blest.

48

THE DYING DOVE.

Oh! that I knew where I might find him! that I might come even to
his seat.—*Job*, 23 : 3.

Oh! mourn not, my turtle—Oh! mourn not, my dove!
Thy deep mellow wailings shall woo back thy love.
Thy blue breast, like heaven, may pour out the lay,
And mourn for thy minion, now far, far away!
The soft winds may bear off thy consummate sighs,
Away from mine own, into other blue skies!
But mourn not, my turtle—Oh! mourn not, my dove!
Thy deep mellow wailings shall woo back thy love.

Thy pinions may bear thee away from my shore,
To mourn where my spirit shall see thee no more!
But where are thy fledglings—thy dear little things?
And are they, like mine, borne away from thy wings?
Ah! many fond hearts have treated like thine!
But none have wounded much deeper than mine!
But mourn not, my turtle—Oh! mourn not, my dove!
Thy deep mellow wailings shall woo back thy love.

I heard thee last evening—this morning—at noon—
And hoped that thy minion might comfort thee soon!
I knew that thy heart was like other loves, torn
Away from those dear ones that never return!
I saw that thy first love none other could be,
And knew that thy strength had departed from thee!
But mourn not, my turtle—Oh! mourn not, my dove!
Thy deep mellow wailings shall woo back thy love.

I saw her descend from the tall dewy limb—
The last tie was broken that bound her to him!
I lent down beside where she bade him adieu,
And gave her three lily-bells charged with the dew!
She drank like an infant three days after birth,
And turned o'er and died on the cold, clammy earth!
I mourned for my turtle—my poor dying dove!
No deep mellow wailings could woo back her love!

THE DYING BEAUTY.

Earth's shadows fly ;
Life, like a dome of many-coloured glass,
Stains the white radiance of eternity,
Until death tramples it to fragments—die,
If thou wouldst be with that which thou dost seek !
Follow where all is fled !—*Adonais.*

Sue died in beauty, like the morn that rose
  In golden glory on the brow of night,
And passed off' gently like the evening's close,
  When day's last steps upon the heavens are bright.
She died in beauty, like the trampled flower
  That yields its fragrance to the passer's feet,
For all her life was as an April shower,
  That kept the tear-drops of her parting sweet.
And like the rainbows of the sunny skies,
  The dew-drop fillet of the brow of even—
That blends its colours as the evening dies—
  Her beauty melted in the light of heaven

She died in softness, like the last sad tone
　　That lingers gently on the midnight ear,
When beauty wanders from her bower alone,
　　And no one answers, but the voice is near.
She died in beauty, like the lonesome dove
　　That seeks her fledglings in the desert air,
And hastes away from out the flowery grove
　　To seek the little ones that nestled there.
And like the humming-bird that seeks the bower,
　　But wings her swiftly from the place away,
And bears the dew-drop from the fading flower—
　　Her spirit wandered to the isle of day.

She died in meekness, like the noiseless lamb
　　When slain upon the altar by the knife,
And lay reclining on her couch so calm,
　　That all who saw her said she still had life.
She died in softness, like the Dorian flute,
　　When heard melodious on the hills at night,
When every voice but that loved one is mute,
　　And all the holy heavens above are bright.
And like the turtle that has lost her love,
　　She hastened quickly from the world to rest;
And passed off gently to the realms above,
　　To reign forever in her FATHER's breast.

She died in glory, like the setting sun,
　　Whose radiance mingles with the azure skies,
That blends so softly they appear but one,
　　And, dying, lives the life that never dies.
She died in sweetness, like the ocean shell,
　　Whose tones are lost upon the moaning deep,
And lay so calmly that we could not tell
　　Her slumber differed from an infant's sleep.

And like the lake, with swans upon its breast,
  The ripples waving to the reedy shore—
She settled softly to her final rest,
  And met her Father to be grieved no more.

TO A CHINA TREE,

WHICH I PLANTED WHEN A BOY.

Suggested by reading the "Old Oaken Bucket," by Woodworth.

Turn all thy dew to splendour, for from thee
The spirit thou lamentest is not gone.—*Adonais.*

How sweet to remember the oaks of my childhood,
  Whose cool shady twilights were haunts of my youth—
The tall wavy pine-tops that hung in the wildwood,
  Whose boughs, in the breeze, sang the music of truth.
And, oh! to remember the China tree growing
  Beside the big road intersecting the state,
Where often I shot with my cross-bow, when snowing,
  The robins that perched on the boughs near the gate.
And shot with my cross-bow—my mulberry cross-bow—
The robins that perched on the boughs near the gate.

When the shadows of night fled away in the morning,
  And the sun robed the mountains and gilded the lands,
I dug up the sprout from the plum-trees adorning,
  And planted it out with my own little hands.

And down on the hill-side—my own little mountain—
In the cove of a rock sat an old speckled goose,
That hissed when I drove her to swim in the fountain
That gushed from the spring like a charger let loose.
And shot with my cross-bow—my mulberry cross-bow—
The robins that perched on the boughs near the gate.

And, oh! how delightful the clear crystal waters
Flowed sporting along through the wood-skirted vale,
Where mother once walked with her dear little daughters,
And combed down their dark glossy locks in the gale.
How fondly I marched with my cross-bow and arrows,
That hung on my arm as I ambled along,
Where, all the day long, I have hunted the sparrows,
And listened, at eve, to the mocking-bird's song.
And shot with my cross-bow—my mulberry cross-bow—
The robins that perched on the boughs near the gate.

'Tis strange how I feel when this childish emotion
Recalls up the past as it were when a boy,
And pictures those features of early devotion,
As perfect as when every sunshine was joy.
The old oakey grove overshadows the China,
As mother once shaded her dear little child,
And the robins now sport with my sister Salina,
As erst with myself ere I came to this wild.
And shot with my cross-bow—my mulberry cross-bow—
The robins that perched on the boughs near the gate.

There are four sombre oaks o'er the well-top reclining,
That nature, in sport, planted out for a shade,
So near equidistant, with artful designing,
That strangers believed them an artful arcade,

Twas there the old scullion suspended the butter,
  While I with my pop-gun, sat high in the tree,
And shot at the robins, while sister would mutter,
  And wistfully look through the boughs up at me.
And shot with my cross-bow—my mulberry cross-bow—
The robins that perched on the boughs near the gate.

Ah! then I was happy—with love overflowing—
  But knew not the value of pleasure by pain,
'Till grief, like the frost, nipped my roses while blowing,
  And tuned up my heart-strings to music again!
And, oh! to remember that day-spring of pleasure,
  Unmixed with the present reflections in pain—
Methinks it were well to look back on the treasure,
  And strive all my life to procure them again.
And shoot with my cross-bow—my mulberry cross-bow—
The robins that perched on the boughs near the gate.

How gladly I looked through the suckle-gemmed valley,
  The grove where the washwoman filled up her tank—
And stood by the well, in the green oakey alley,
  And turned down the old cedar bucket and drank.
But farewell, ye oaks! and the trees of my childhood!
  And all the bright scenes appertaining to joy!
I think of ye often, away in this wildwood,
  But never shall be as I was when a boy.
Nor shoot with my cross-bow—my mulberry cross-bow—
The robins that perched on the boughs near the gate.

TO MY MOTHER.

WRITTEN WHILE SOJOURNING IN A DISTANT LAND.

The words of a man's mouth are as deep waters, and the well-spring of wisdom as a flowing brook.—*Proverbs of Solomon.*

I.

When my last summer's sun was spent with thee,
I thought to find another friend on earth,
A dream untold—a dream it is I see !
Then, lovely mother ! author of my birth !
Thou who didst teach me innocence and mirth !
To seek thy like is searching the unknown !
For who, when found, could be of so much worth ?
And who has been so kind to me, mine own !
Who call'st me thy dear child as if I were not grown !

II.

And I have been two years or more away
From thee, and still my feelings are not changed !
I love thee as if absent but one day,
For nothing earthly have my thoughts estranged !
I have, with beauty, many smiles exchanged,
And fed my soul on sentiments divine ;
But these are trifles—they have nothing changed—
For I am, as it were, a spark of thine,
And that which thou dost own, the same sweet things are
mine.

III.

My mother! still I feel the day we parted
Fresh in my remembrance—thy good advice
Was like relief unto the broken-hearted—
A precious incense from a sacrifice !
That caused upon my soul a sun to rise,
That ne'er shall set!—for, since the day I left,
I have adored thine absence—nor mine eyes
Been tearless but in sleep!—The wing is cleft
That made my journey—else thou wert no longer reft !

IV.

Thus basking in thy kindness, I proceed
In my devotion—and, with love that flows
From an unbridled current, teem and bleed
In my soul's worship, till my kindness knows
No barrier—feels no bounds—but onward goes.
Like a majestic river which sweeps down
All opposition—ending where it rose
In the soul's ocean—that it may redown
To make me happy—crown me with a righteous crown.

V.

Those scenes which I would willingly descry,
Are far beyond the mountains—but these strings
Are not awakened from a theme so high
To sing perspective—they are trivial things—
Which I can see at pleasure—that which brings
Contentment, mixed with sorrow, hath its source
In the heart's fiery mountain—*there* it springs
From an unfathomed fountain—and its course
Wends onward to the soul to spend affection's force.

VI.

There is no voice to mortal ears so sweet
As chidings from a mother's fervent love ;
And that dear kindness which I used to greet,
Now pours upon me as from heaven above !
But I have left thine ark—a faithful dove—
Of all within most surely to return—
And be it long or late, where'er I rove,
I never will forget my native bourne,
The place where thou didst teach me that I loved to learn.

VII.

I taste much that is sweet, and hear the voice
Of pleasantness salute mine ear—I feel
As if my hopes would soon rejoice
In their completion, and my future weal
Be centred in a heart—but not of steel !
As if transported on the wings of bliss,
I hold thee near me—seal thee with a seal
Of unrelenting kindness—with a kiss
Which is not of this world—to cancel all distress.

VIII.

My mother ! may thy joys on earth increase,
As did the widow's cruise of precious oil ;
May all thy paths be paths of perfect peace,
To lead thee o'er an unadulterate soil.
May weal and wisdom crown thy daily toil,
And learn, like Deborah, what thou shouldst know,
And have revealed that which shall never spoil,
As was the voice that went to Jericho,
Beyond the oak of Ophrah unto old Shiloh.

IX.

Man's life is as a shadow!—Let thy sun—
The chastener of my spirit—shine again!
Let that which I had long ago begun,
Take root and flourish—let my heart obtain
Some recompense for absence and for pain!
That I may come at the appointed hour,
Enthroned in love—that I may always gain
Thy confidence—*then* will my soul have power
To pour down on thy latter age a bounteous shower.

X.

May God be with thee—heaven dispense thee aid—
That all around and over thee may shine!
May life be precious—death a pleasant shade—
To lead thee unto blessedness divine!
And may no less be granted unto thine,
That when resolved to pass from life to death—
From death to life—no longer to repine—
Which beams upon me with awakened faith—
May we unite in heaven to breathe each other's breath.

EVENING.

God bless the evening! Glorious are the hills!
And happy are the mountains, and the seas,
At this devoted hour! Glorious heavens!
The silent, awful depths of solitude,
Where nature worships God alone—how grand!

How glorious are the thunderings forth of that
Bright scripture, where the everlasting hills
Are auditors to God, and where they stand
To hear the repercussive thunder speak
The fulness of his glory, when he comes
In gladness and rejoicing, horsed upon
The lightnings in the whirlwinds of his might!
The awful grandeur of thy presence fills
Me with adoring! For the cloudless skies
Are beautiful, and nature rides triumphant
Through the opening gates of heaven, and leads
The soul into the mercy-seat of God, to live
And learn the anthems of the moon and stars,
And sing the hallelujahs of the blest.
For all the kingdoms of the earth are filled
With gladness, and the clustering island-clouds
Are throned above creation, like to ships
Of gold upon cerulean seas!—For all
The merchandise of visionary bliss
Is setting sail for heaven; and now the dews
Of ocean are like angel locks on high,
As if advancing to the isles of love,
And thus my spirit fills!—*then*, let me say,
God bless the evening! 'Tis the solemn time
To love with rapture—when all else is still—
When life keeps music with the song of birds,
And with the waterfalls that praise the Lord.
When love gives all its energies to hope,
And feeds upon those splendour-bursts that fill
The animated soul! yea, when the truths
Of heaven are written on the wonder-works
Of God, and when the ocean drinks the sun
In glory, and exults beneath the stars.
When nature makes her mistress of the earth—

The stranger seeks the inn—and the laborer
Returns from his hire—when the lover calls
Upon his mistress—and, when God is seen
Apparent in the works that he has made.
May God Almighty bless the evening! bless
The everlasting, silent evening! when
The Lord ascended on the Mount to talk
With Moses and Elias—when he prayed
And Peter slept—and when the Jews refused
Him entertainment!—when he taught them all
The way into his Father's house; and when
His passion was too great for man to bear!
And when the glorious star appeared in heaven,
To herald Jesus Christ on earth!—when all
Was filled with harmony—Elijah came
From Cherith—when the mountain rocks were rent,
And God Almighty's "*still small voice*" was heard
In heaven's repercussive thunder!—The time
When dear Almeda met me by the sea,
And paid the sacred vows of love!—and when
The angel of the Lord appeared in heaven,
Descended on the rainbows of the skies—
And with her soul ascended into bliss.
But still, God bless the evening! We shall meet
Again, beside still waters, where there is
Nor day nor night! for glory hath no need
Of sunshine,—for the face of God doth light
His kingdom, where eternity shall roll
To that immortal morning, when the soul
Shall feed upon Jehovah, as upon
The spirit-bursts of that bright one, whose joy
Is now unspeakable and full of love.

MAN'S LIFE.

He cometh forth like a flower, and is cut down; he fleeth like a shadow
and continueth not.—*Job*, 14: 2.

His birth is like the little star
  That bursts through evening's shade alone,
Till thunder-clouds are seen afar.
  And, passing, soon its beams are gone.
And when expiring twilight dies,
  And other stars her beams accost,
She melts into the distant skies,
  And evening weeps her Pleiade lost.

His youth is like the little star
  That ushers in the morning light;
But melts beneath the fiery car
  That rolls upon her portals bright.
As over morning's radiant hues
  A sickly grayish mist appears.
That ripens into falling dews,
  And weeps itself away to tears.

His youth is like the little isle
  That bowed beneath her canopy,
As Venus caught her sunny smile,
  When rising from the foaming sea.
And like that isle, which saw her glide,
  The seasons waiting quick return—
His heart is washed by every tide,
  And, ocean like, must ever mourn!

His youth is like the morning calm
　That steals upon exulting day,
Whose wings are laden down with balm,
　As tempests blow them all away.
And thus his manhood's little weal,
　When passion's storms are gathering round,
Lies furled beneath the poisoned steel,
　That kills before he feels the wound.

His life is like the mountain stream
　That wends along through hillocks steep,
That wider grows while others teem,
　Till lost in ocean's briny deep.
And thus man's life renews—decays—
　Through time's eventful changes free,
Though many shoals obstruct his ways,
　And ends like rivers meet the sea.

THE VOICE OF THE EXILE

Yes!
I have asked that dreadful question of the hills
That look eternal ; of the flowing streams
That lucid flow forever ; of the stars,
Amid whose fields of azure my raised spirit
Hath trod in glory : all were dumb ;—
　　　　　We shall meet
Again, Clemanthe !—*Ion.*

Bring home the child—the child of love—
　And let her cure my beating heart of pain !
Oh ! let my hand reach forth the desert dove,
　And bring her safely to my ark again !

6

For now my heart is breaking in my breast—
Bring home the turtle to her native nest!

Bring home the child—the voice appeals
 To thee, whose memory never more shall be
Bright with the sunshine that forever seals
 The undimmed fountains of my soul for thee!
The reed that cannot stay the torrent's course,
Must die beneath the glory of its force!

Bring home the child—the tuneful bird—
 The April dove that cannot coo in vain—
Oh! bring her safely where she never heard
 The soft sweet lyre she may not hear again!
Bring back the turtle to the heart that lies
A living remnant of our broken ties!

Bring home the child—here let her rest
 As sunshine to the chaos of my heart!
For now it rolls within my darkened breast,
 As earth before the veil was rent apart
That made the universe, around us seen,
Rush into life two brighter worlds between.

Bring home the child—there is around
 The heart that calls upon thy startled ear,
An untold music, whose eternal sound
 Comes forth like wailings from that sepulchre,
Wherein is laid all that the heart loves most,
Of whose deep moan this music is the ghost!

Bring home the child—there is no voice
 To mortal ears like that unheeded tone,
Whose music makes the very heart rejoice,
 And in the echo leaves it more alone!

A sound that gushes from my heart to be
A stream within thy soul's eternity !

Bring home the child—the absent dove—
  The wandering Pleiade to her sky again !
Oh ! bring her safely unto so much love—
  The sweetest heart that ever broke in vain !
And in the garden, watered with our tears,
Plant out the roses of our earlier years !

Bring home the child—the heart is broken
  That nerved the accents of my harp unstrung !
The last sad word that ever shall be spoken,
  Is dying now upon my faltering tongue !
Go forth, sad voice ! another harp shall be
The untold music of thy witchery !

Bring home the child—no other shell
  Shall sigh melodious unto thee again !
For that deep agony which bade me tell
  My sorrows, is the last inviting strain
That ever shall upon my harp-strings die,
While yon eternal sun shall roll on high !

Bring home the child—yes, let her come
  As leaps the roebuck on the hills at even !
Here let her lie upon my breast at home,
  As rest the pinions of the dove in heaven !
Oh ! let her voice upon my spirit break,
As break the ripples on the reedy lake.

Bring home the child—the last sad chord
  That ever shall be stricken now is strung !
For all that ever mortal felt or heard
  Is dying now upon my faltering tongue !

The storm that wrecked my flindered barque shall be
The breeze that shall conduct my soul to thee!

Bring home the child—Oh! never more,
    In this fond bosom, shall such sorrows roll!
The last dark wave that lashed affection's shore,
    Is pausing now upon my weary soul!
The syren mistress of its tides shall be
A lamp hung out beyond eternity!

SONG OF ADORATION TO GOD.

"In that day shall this song be sung in the land.—*Isaiah* 26: 1.

Lord! in the Temple of thy love,
Bowed in thy radiance from above,
Mantled with thy redeeming light,
And ordered in thy steps aright;
Let the soft wooings of thy wings
Shadow the music of my strings.

Lord! like the desert fount that flowed
Fast by the feet of Hagar bowed,
Thirsting amid the desert wild
She wandered with her outcast child—
Oh! pour upon me thy soft beams,
And circle me with heavenly streams.

If, in the whirlwinds of the sea,
A prayer is offered up to thee ;
If thou art on the page of night,
Written in syllables of light ;
And if thy hands have made the sun,
Lord ! tell me what thou hast not done !

If thou hast ceiled the heavens with blue,
And laced them with the morning dew ;
If thou hast placed the stars of light
Upon the curtains of the night ;
And if thy hands have made them ways,
Lord ! let me offer up my praise !

If, from the chaos of old Night,
The stars were whispered into flight !
If, when another word was given,
The sun stood on the hills of heaven !
And if these things were made for me,
Lord ! tell me what to do for thee !

Lo ! if the universe hath words,
And they are spoken by the birds !
And if the rivers roll along
In the deep eloquence of song ;
If these have been since time began,
Lord ! what should be the praise of man !

If night doth prophesy to night
The language of the morning light ;
And if the morning doth appear
To whisper to the evening near ;
And if these things pour forth to thee,
Lord ! what should not be said by me !

6 6

Are not the songsters of the grove
Vocal with thy redeeming love ?
Are not the burning stars of even
The members of thy church in heaven ?
And if they are but lamps to me,
Lord ! teach me how to worship thee.

FAITH.

FAITH is the flower that blooms unseen
By mountains of immortal green —
A hoped-for harvest in the skies,
In which the reaper never dies —
A tree to which the power is given
To lift its branches into heaven ;
And from whose boughs of gorgeous fruit
A loftier tree shall take its root.

Lord ! we are grafted into thine,
When broken off from Adam's vine ;
And so, from that degenerate tree,
We grow into the life of thee !
For, by the prunings of thy word,
Are we then purged into the Lord ;
And like Mount Zion we shall stand
The Temples of our native land.

Lord ! if the stars should take their flight,
And vanish from the halls of night ;
And if the morning should appear,
And vanish from the evening near ;

And if the rivers should run dry,
And every flower that decks them die ;
And if the world should cease to be—
I would not lose my trust in thee.

SACRED SONG.

By the rivers of Babylon we sat down and wept, when we remembered
Zion.—*Bible.*

By Zion's sweet waters we wept,
    And sprinkled our bosoms with tears !
In Kedron's dark valley we slept,
    And, waking, outnumbered her years !
The pilgrim that never hath sighed,
    Shall tremble while gazing on thee,
And mourn that his Shiloh hath died,
    Ere Jacob's young damsels were free !

But Barak's ten thousand are gone,
    And Tabor shall tremble no more,
Where Necho caused Judah to mourn,
    And scattered his people before !
Thy chariots, Sisera ! are gone !
    And Canaan shall flourish once more,
When Shiloh shall gather his own,
    And people this desolate shore.

MORNING HYMN.

"LET THERE BE LIGHT!" And lo! there stole
  From out the womb of Darkness, light!
A flood of glory circled round the soul,
  And rent the curtains of primeval night!
Through all the vast immensities of space
  A glorious light streamed up eternity!
And, bursting through all chaos, sought its place
  In the bright islands of the earth and sea!

"LET THERE BE LIGHT!" And from the abyss
  Of Darkness gushed the Eternal's smile!
And flying through all Nature, came to this,
  And gave the firmament another isle!
For Time was as Eternity is now,
  Till that immortal light was given,
Whose smile of gladness from Jehovah's brow
  Lit up the confines of the realms of heaven!

"LET THERE BE LIGHT!" And from the slime
  Of that immortal sea, whose wave is love,
The Maker gave existence unto Time,
  By smiling on his workmanship above.
And, rising from that great supernal power,
  The same sweet smile ascends the sky,
As from the birth of that auspicious hour
  Ten thousand worlds were sentinelled on high.

EVENING HYMN.

Unto thee, O Lord, do I lift my soul.—*Psalms*, 25: 1.

Lord of the stars of night! thy love
Is ever beaming from above!
Thy name is written in the sky,
In the bright lunar realms on high!

They are appointed to be bright,
And to make glad the halls of night;
And, from the chambers of the west,
To beckon me away to rest.

Lord! if the realms of endless space
Are thine eternal dwelling-place,
Surely thou art upon the light
Of that bright seraph of the night.

And if thou art upon that sphere,
I know that thou art with me here;
And if thou art the soul of me,
Lord! what should I not do for thee!

Then, in the fulness of thy power,
Pour on the offering of this hour
The healing incense of thy love,
And lift my sacrifice above.

HYMN TO THE DEITY.

Heal me, O Lord, and I shall be healed: and save me, and I shall be
saved : for thou art my praise.—*Jeremiah*, 17 : 14.

Lord ! let the rivers of thy love
Pour out upon me from above !
Let the bright waves of glory roll
Around the sanctuary of my soul !

Let not the island-clouds that lie
On the pavilion of the sky,
Gather around thy dwelling-place,
And hide the glory of thy face !

Thou art upon the raging seas,
And on the whispers of the breeze ;
And in the lightnings of the sky,
And in the firmament on high !

Thou art upon the mighty hills,
And in the music of the rills ;
And in the whirlwinds of the sea,
And in the voice that speaks to thee !

Thou art upon the darkest night,
And in the brightest of the light ;
And in the place where none can dwell—
For thou art in the depths of hell !

Thy foot-prints are the stars of even
To lead my spirit up to heaven!
And every grain of sand must see
The truth of it as well as me.

For, in the silence of thy voice,
The very thunders doth rejoice!
And even the meekness of thy might
Is greater than the solar light!

Thus seeing that thy home is here,
And feeling that thy voice is near;
And knowing what thy strength must be,—
I offer up my prayer to thee!

DRINK AND AWAY.

There is a beautiful rill in Barbary received into a large basin, which bears the name signifying " Drink and Away," from the great danger of meeting with rogues and assassins.—*Dr. Shaw.*

If the stranger should pass over Barbary's waters,
There is one little rill that may tempt him to stay,
For the nectar that makes it so sweet to her daughters,
Is the warning that tells him to " Drink and Away."
Then the words that are written, dear pilgrim! rely on,
For no joy in this world should entice thee to stay—
If the earth have no waters like those are in Zion,
Oh! think of her fountains—then " Drink and Away."

If the soul should be parched by that hot raging fever
That dries up the heart in this friendless abode,
Oh! forget not the hopes of the righteous forever,
For the stars are the footsteps that lead thee to God !
And the voice that shall never be lost to the stranger,
Though the fountains of Pleasure may tempt him to stay—
Is the voice of the Lord that shall guard him from danger
When friends all forsake him—then "Drink and Away!"

But put not thy trust in this world's shining river,
For no heart by its waters was ever made whole ;
And the stranger that seeks for its virtue shall never,
No, never in Lethe find rest for his soul.
And when broken of rest by that cool shady mountain,
Whose height over all is the beacon of day,
Then drink from the depths of that pure holy fountain
Whose warning shall never say—" Drink and Away."

SONG OF THE DYING SOLDIER.

THE fountains are streaming, are streaming
   With music, dear Mary! for thee !
Thy cheeks, too, are beaming, are beaming
   With sadness, dear Mary! for me!
     For we never shall meet
     On that cool mossy seat,
Where wild weeds are growing, are growing !
     But, although we must part,
     Thou shalt dwell with my heart,
Where rose-buds are blowing, are blowing!

Oh! hush then thy weeping, thy weeping
  With sorrow, dear Mary! for me!
My dark locks are steeping, are steeping
  In warm tears, dear Mary! for thee!
    For we never shall meet
    On that cool mossy seat,
Where wild weeds are growing, are growing!
    But, alas! do not care—
    Thou shalt dwell with me there,
Where rose-buds are blowing, are blowing.

Thy young cheeks are fading, are fading
  With sorrow, dear Mary! for me!
For Death now is shading, is shading
  My spirit, dear Mary! from thee!
    For we never shall meet
    On that cool mossy seat,
Where wild weeds are growing, are growing!
    Then adieu!—we must part—
    Thou shalt dwell with my heart,
Where we now are going—are going!

TO INEZ DE GEORGIA,

ON PRESENTING ME WITH A PIONEY IN FULL BLOOM.

Oh! when time shall break the chain
  That this precious gift doth bind
Round my beating heart again,
  As mine arms around thee twined—

7

Will this same Pioney bloom
In thy fond remembrance, dear!
And re-thrill thee, when the tomb
Shall deny my presence here?

But perchance thy spirit knows
That this undiminished fire
Shall forbid our tombs to close,
Till our hopes are lifted higher.
For its brightness shall be given,
As when stars rejoin the sky,
To my beating heart, when heaven
Shall return my soul on high.

As yon pearly clouds that lie,
As my head upon thy breast,
As if angel's locks on high—
That can find no sweeter rest;
And like Nature's soft repose
On yon deep unruffled sea,
When life's chafing storms shall close—
Shall my spirit sleep with thee.

SONG.

GEORGIA WATERS.

On thy waters, thy sweet valley waters,
Oh! Georgia! how happy were we!
When thy daughters, thy sweet-smiling daughters,
Once gathered sweet-william for me.

Oh! thy wildwood, thy dark shady wildwood
   Had many bright visions for me ;
For my childhood, my bright rosy childhood
   Was cradled, dear Georgia! in thee.

On thy mountains, thy green purple mountains,
   The seasons are waiting on thee ;
And thy fountains, thy clear crystal fountains
   Are making sweet music for me.
Oh! thy waters, thy sweet valley waters
   Are dearer than any to me ;
For thy daughters, thy sweet-smiling daughters,
   Oh! Georgia! give beauty to thee.

TO LITTLE LIZA IN HEAVEN.

Many waters cannot quench love, neither can the floods drown it ; if a man would give all the substance of his house for love, it would utterly be contemned.--*Solomon's Songs.*

   WHITHER, my absent one !
Oh! whither hast thy dove-like beauty fled ?
Thou pure bright gem! that leavest thy pearls alone,
   To join earth's mighty dead !
And has thy soul into heaven been led,
'To dwell where we that have been shall be ?
Where those that mourn shall rejoice with thee ?

Whither, young frightened dove !
My long-loved Liza ! hast thy spirit flown ?
By what soft hand hast thou been led above ?
        Oh ! make thy passport known,
And soothe my heart with thy cherub tone !
That when my soul shall ascend into rest,
The soft blue heavens may pillow my breast,
And meeting thee—hallowed—divine—
The angels may mingle my spirit with thine !

        Whither, since life was new,
When thou wert star-like under heaven above—
A light undimmed though seen from distant view—
        Hast thou been borne, my love ?
        Whither, through burning skies,
From woodbine alcoves where our joys were fleet—
Where matin song-birds wooed away our sighs—
        More sorrowful than sweet—
Oh ! whither shall my spirit track thy feet,
Sweet heir unto blessedness more than divine ?
A brighter star than those which tune their spheres
        To heaven's deep roundelay !
        Whither, from many tears,
O ! whither dost thy spirit wing its way,
To tune my harp unto glory like thine ?
        Whither, with angels, dear !
A star that shone above life's fearful sea—
        The brightest gem of even !
Oh ! wherefore hast thou left my spirit here,
        To make thy home in heaven !

        Gone, evermore from me !
Oh ! loved one ! gone forevermore !

For thou shalt never be,
As thou wert once, upon this barren shore!
Oh! never more at noon,
Nor eventide, wilt thou resume the song!
And never in June,
Be seen beside still waters, where the birds
Were all asleep!
Nor whisper unto me those holy words
That make my spirit weep!
But long—long!
Oh! longer than my soul shall live to tell—
Wilt thou ascend to rest!
And there with thy Jehovah dwell,
And live upon his breast!
For never, never more,
While yon eternal sun shall roll on high—
The moon reign mistress of the sea—
The stars sing hallelujahs in the sky—
Nor while eternity shall roll
To reap enjoyment for the soul—
Wilt thou be seen upon this shore!
Oh! this hath made me sad!
But when life's sorrows shall be o'er,
I will be glad;
And have my troubles swallowed in the sea
Of endless life, great God! with thee.

THE MOTHER'S LAMENT.

COMPOSED ON THE DEATH OF MY SISTER'S CHILD.

"I shall go to him, but he shall not return to me."

Oh! they tell me not to sigh,
  And they tell me not to moan ;
But were all this world to die,
  I would not be so alone !
Oh! they cannot comfort me,
  For their bounties all are vain—
And the joys that were to be,
  Cannot come to me again !
If their Gilead could be brought
  From beyond the stars at even,
They might pacify my thought—
  There is rest for me in heaven.

Oh! there is no balm for me,
  And my tears must ever flow !
Though they seem like grief to thee,
  They are antidotes to wo.
He was all my sun by day,
  He was all my stars by night ;
And however rough the way,
  He was always my delight.
For he lived upon my breast,
  Like the first bright star of even
When it wanes upon the west—
  There is rest for me in heaven.

And the spring may come again,
　And embrace the little spot,
And refresh the sons of men—
　But my babe will know it not!
Like the mateless dove that hies
　From her desolated nest,
I must take me to the skies,
　Where my little one shall rest!
For the woes that compass me,
　Are like waves when rudely driven
Round an island in the sea—
　There is rest for me in heaven.

Though the flocks may all be seen
　In the valleys far away,
And the mountains look as green
　As the sunny isles of day;
Though the spring may pass away,
　And the summer take its place,
And the autumn be as gay—
　I shall never see his face!
I shall never see his eyes
　In the stillness of the even—
I shall meet him in the skies—
　There is rest for me in heaven.

Though my spirit live to thirst
　For the healing wells of love,
And my bosom come to burst
　For the fountains from above;
Though the rivers of my grief
　Shall like Siloah's waters flow,
And shall bring me no relief
　In this trying world below;

Though my beating heart may break,
    And its tender chords be riven
By this sorrow for thy sake—
    There is rest for me in heaven.

Though the sun shall come to fall
    From his attitude on high;
And the stars beneath the pall
    Of his darkness wrapped to die;
Though the earth shall come to boast
    Of her grave-clothes in the clouds;
And the universe be lost
    In the darkest of all shrouds;
Though the hand of thunder hurls
    Every fragment, newly riven,
To the crush of falling worlds—
    There is rest for me in heaven.

But my sorrows soon shall cease,
    And my spirit then shall be
In that blessed isle of peace,
    Where there is no grief with *thee!*
Oh! but would you have me smile?
    Then ascend the wings of morn—
Fly away to that bright isle,
    Where the sun himself was born—
Bring me back the babe that made
    All my rosy paths so even—
Bring me back the early dead—
    There is rest for me in heaven.

There is joy for those that weep,
    There is joy for those that die;
There are harvests there to reap,
    In the heavens above on high!

There are fields forever green,
　There are rivers never dry ;
'There are heavenly hills between
　The bright valleys of the sky !
Where the last celestial beam
　Of the sun to chaos driven,
Shall announce the opening gleam
　Of my rest with thee in heaven.

BURIAL OF THE INDIAN CHILD.

I SATE down where Lena was weeping,
　Who mourned that her parents were wild ;
I asked her whose infant was sleeping—
　She told me 'twas Atala's child !—
The rock-born, dear ermine ! to-morrow
　The wood-nymphs shall pillow his head !
I asked her—she told me, in sorrow,
　That Atala's baby was dead !
　　　I would suckle him now,
　　　But his cold winter brow
　　Is sleeping away from her eye—
　　　I would suckle him now,
　　　But her young dove must die !
　　　　Lullaby ! lullaby !

Oh ! pale face ! thy dark locks are shading
　The big tears that warmed them before !
Thy cold, livid lips too are fading—
　The big light shall warm them no more !

I saw her baptize him with fountains
  Of new milk that ran from her breast ;
But now she is gone o'er the mountains,
  And Onee must lay down to rest !
    I would suckle him now,
    But his cold winter brow
  Is sleeping away from her eye—
    I would suckle him now,
    But her young dove must die ?
      Lullaby ! lullaby !

She rose while her fingers were wreathing
  The roses that hung on his head,
And said, while her accents were breathing,
  'Tis here we shall make down his bed !
The bright dews that morning were weeping
  And balming each rose-bud that grew
So bright where her eagle was sleeping,
  The place where she bade him adieu !
    I would suckle him now,
    But his cold winter brow
  Is now sleeping away from her eye—
    I would suckle him now,
    But her young dove must die !
      Lullaby ! lullaby !

She knelt down—her tresses were flowing—
  And buried him low in the rocks !
And while her young features were glowing,
  She wiped down her tears with her locks !
The big light she worshipped was beaming
  The roses that mantled his grave ;
She left him—with tear drops as streaming—
  With One that she trusted could save.

I would suckle him now,
But her cold winter brow
Is sleeping away from her eye—
I would suckle him now,
But her young dove must die!
Lullaby! lullaby!

SONG.

WITH my head upon thy breast,
And my hand within thine own—
Ah! 'twould give me sweeter rest
Than upon an ivory throne.

With my hand upon thine own,
And thy bosom turned from me—
Ah! 'twould leave me more alone
Than an island in the sea.

So thy name shall ever rest
In my memory still for years,
Till upon some other breast
I may wipe away my tears.

THE HARPER.

Who think it solitude to be alone?—*Young.*

A HARPER who had left his native land,
 A land above all other lands for love—
And one that struck his lyre with David's hand,
 Sat down lamenting with his thoughts above:

> Tell her she sleeps afar,
> In that lone silent rest,
> Beyond the western star—
> Where all are haply blest!

> Tell her my days are past,
> And all my hopes have fled!
> For song alone can last,
> When those that sung are dead!

> Tell her the skies are blue,
> That roses, too, are sweet—
> That friends are very few,
> And we no more shall meet!

> Tell her my harp alone
> Can soothe this silent grief,
> Since that dear one is gone
> That gave me such relief!

Tell her my days are fleet,
    That song must soon be o'er—
For she who made it sweet,
    Shall hear me sing no more!

Tell her that song is sweet
    Because her heart is true—
Tell her that we shall meet
    No more on earth—Adieu!

       I saw him sadly weep
The deep warm tears that sorrow bade him shed,
And sink into himself with silence deep,
And mourn about his long lost Lenah dead!

       The dove that builds her nest
In garden cedar, where, from morn till night,
The loved ones meet, had more secluded rest
Than this same sad—this broken-hearted wight!

       But now his soul is free
As that sweet harp that he had often strung!
The willow boughs bend over by the sea,
Where never more shall that sweet song be sung!

       And, often, it is said,
At night, when other things are all asleep,
The sea-winds moan about his lonely bed,
And spirits gather round his harp to weep!

8

SONG.

Come take all my jewels and lie down, my dove!
And rest on my bosom, my own dearest love!
Come lie on the roses—the fairest of spring—
And see the white swan from the rivers take wing.

Come rest where the wild running streams hyaline
Are borne far away from the limpets that shine—
Come rest where the mountains have valleys between,
And lie on the velvet that robes them with green.

Come lie down, my dearest! with peace in my arms,
And give me to banquet all night on thy charms!
Oh! come with thy music—with words that console—
And light the dark midnight that broods on my soul!

Oh! come to my bosom—come lie on my breast—
And feed me with love till my spirit shall rest!
Oh! come to my thyme-beds besprinkled with dew,
And cheer up the heart that is breaking for you.

SONG.

Oh! come away, my gentle one!
　　At midnight come to me,
And rest upon my breast alone,
　　In moonlight by the sea.

Oh! get you there among the vines,
   'Tis light enough for me—
For when alone thy beauty shines,
   'Tis moonlight by the sea.

Oh! come again, my early love!
   And meet me when the skies,
And every star that shines above,
   Are swimming in thine eyes.
The moon shall hear each tender tone,
   The stars above shall see
Thee lie upon my breast alone,
   In moonlight by the sea.

Oh! come again, my dearest love!
   At midnight, when the eyes
Of vigils are upturned above,
   To gaze upon the skies—
At night alone should love be heard,
   And thou alone with me,
To dwell upon each whispered word,
   In moonlight by the sea.

Oh! come again, my fairest love!
   When every thought is deep,
And meet me when the stars above
   Have sung the moon to sleep.
And will you come?—Oh! tell me, sweet!
   And will you come to me?
For, oh! it is such joy to meet
   In moonlight by the sea.

SONG.

BLESSED of heaven! thy home shall be
In the bright green isle of my love for thee,
When thy form shall rest on my spirit bright,
Like the silver moon on the starry night ;
When thy voice shall float on my soul awake,
Like the gentle swan on the azure lake—
Blessed of heaven! thy home shall be
In the bright green isle of my love for thee.

Blessed of heaven! thy home shall be
In the bright green isle of my love for thee,
When the pale cold lips thou hast caused to sigh,
On the heavenly blush of thy cheeks shall lie ;
When the tears that gush from my soul so wide,
In the dark long strans of thy locks shall hide—
Blessed of heaven! thy home shall be
In the bright green isle of my love for thee.

Blessed of heaven! thy home shall be
In the bright green isle of my love for thee,
When the heart that beats in my aching breast,
By the tender pulse of thine own shall rest ;
When my lips shall breathe of thyself alone,
And thy tender heart shall be all mine own—
Blessed of heaven! thy home shall be
In the bright green isle of my love for thee.

TO MY MOTHER.

Thou hast been to me, in mine hours of grief,
The healing cordial of sublime relief.
Thou hast been to me, in mine hours of thirst,
The cool outpourings of affections nursed.
    And 'tis not that I see thee with an eye
More dark and sightless than I had of yore;
    And 'tis not that my feelings, by-and-by,
Shall feel less tender than they were before.
    And 'tis not that my bosom hath no care,
That I do not for thee more often mourn;
    But time hath taught me with myself to bear,
And brave those things which youth could not have borne.
And 'tis not that I yearn for thee the less,
Or live unmoved by that strange tenderness;
    And 'tis not that my heart has callous grown,
That I do not complain for one so dear!
    For I have felt what man hath never known,
And wept when no one saw me shed a tear!
And not that I have lost one tender feeling,
But that such love was past my youth's concealing;
And that I now have o'er me more control
Than when a child—when I had too much soul.
As well may Time attempt to drain the sea,
As waste one atom of my love for thee.

THE DYING POET TO HIS CHILD.

Save me, O God, for the waters have come in unto my soul,—*Psalms*, 69 ; 1.

THE ball that wounds the mated dove,
　　Inflicts but little pain ;
But fortune stabbed by blighted love,
　　Must leave the victim slain !
The storm that wrings the towering oak,
　　May crush it long to lie ;
But Fate can wield a keener stroke—
　　My little babe, good-by !

The careless foot may crush the worm,
　　And feel no inward pang ;
But he that tramps the adder's form,
　　May dread each poisoned fang !
And he that trusts the broken reed,
　　Shall feel it pierce and try
The heart that must forever bleed—
　　My little babe, good-by !

As dew-drops pure and chaste as snow
　　In falling may be changed ;
So, hearts oft chided—racked by wo—
　　Will soon become estranged !
The dog that meets with constant blows
　　Will shun his master's eye ;
And snap the hand that food bestows—
　　My little babe, good-by !

Thy years are not enough to know
 The sorrows that await,—
In friendship's garb doth envy go
 To haunt thee long and late !
Then task the vows that men may give,
 As future years roll nigh,
For I am now too sick to live—
 My little babe, good-by !

And though mine eyes may never see
 Thy face on earth, my love !
Yet, God will fix some plan for me
 To meet my child above !
This consolation soothes my plaint,
 And cancels every sigh ;
Or else my heart would burst or faint—
 My little babe, good-by !

And now upon life's stormy sea
 My weary barque sails on,
But Death shall soon blow down the tree
 That stands on earth alone !
And now dark visions intercept
 My soul from every eye !
But all is done—as Jacob wept—
 My little babe, good-by !

ODE TO THE MISSISSIPPI.

Thou " *Father of Waters !*" thou million in one !
Oh ! speak from the North where thy travels begun,
And tell me the first with thyself to unite,
Who walked down the valley like lovers at night,
Till thou, with thy freedom majestic and deep,
Bestrode like an emperor walking in sleep.

And where is the strength that can sever the bands
That bind them in union from far distant lands ?
So strange in complexion, in climate, and light,
Like soldiers enlisted for Freedom to fight !
Who started their marching ere Adam was born,
And never shall stop till Eternity's morn.

Thus endless, majestic, supreme, and divine !
They never grow callous by age or decline !
But ever uniting and shaking of hands,
They walk down in love through the low valley-lands ;
And however strange in complexion at sight,
They always commingle and ever unite.

'Tis strange that so many should flow into one,
And rush down the valley like light from the sun !
'Tis stranger to think that the savage and free
Should walk the same road to their homes in the sea !
Which proves that the lion and lamb shall be friends,
And earth, in a time, to its uttermost ends.

He came with Eternity—flows with its tide—
And none can say ought or his wonders deride—
He opens his breast like a schoolboy at play,
And bears the world's merchandise freely away!
He looks in the moonlight as wide as the sea,
And rolls up his billows in tempests as free!

Then wind thee along to the climes of the sun—
Thou bottomless king! to Eternity run!
The wild, like Manoah, hath prayed for a child,
And thou art the Sampson, the king of the wild!
And, like unto Ishmael, around thee shall spring
A kingdom of nations to call thee their king,

We look on thy bosom, but cannot control
The terror that strikes from the heart to the soul!
We know thee unique in the East or the West,
Who look'st in a calm like a lion at rest!
We give thee the praise—then adieu to the wild
That brought forth a son called Eternity's child.

TO IRENE.

THE gentle dove prepares her young no food,
  Nor does she teach them how she built her nest,
Nor how upon her new laid eggs to brood—
  These things they know—are they not doubly blest?

The tuneful linnet pours her matin tone
    As did her sire in Eden's rosy bower—
Yea, tends her young till they are fledged and flown,
    With all the kindness of that happy hour.

'Tis thus, sweet lady! I would nurse and tend
    To bathe thy pinions in exalted flight,
And strive with thine to make my actions blend,
    As two deep rivers when they first unite.

Or thrills, like dew-drops on some gentle flower,
    When left alone, they shine like starry light ;
But when they mingle—by some heavenly power—
    They make but one, a thousand times more bright.

'Tis thus our feelings into one shall flow,
    Like silver dew-drops of the morn and even,
Till two fond hearts make one on earth below,
    And that bright one as deep as earth from heaven.

As two deep fountains all their rills unite,
    In some wide valley where sweet roses blow,
So shall our beings blend with one delight,
    And from two brooklets make life's river flow.

THE MOTHER CHIDING HER FIRST BORN.

Touch not the baby—let her lie—
    And in her cradle sleep;
But brush away each restive fly,
    But do not make her weep.

Her flaxen hair—her snow-white breast—
 Her silken lashes fine—
Her coral lips, so calm at rest,
 Breathe something so divine.

" Oh, mother ! let me give one kiss,
 And I will go away ?"
" Yes, take it, dear ! nor act amiss,
 And get thee off to play.
Find some cool shade among the vine
 In yon sequestered dale,
Where wanton winds the boughs entwine
 In every freshening gale."

" Oh, mother ! let me kiss once more
 That sweet and pretty bird ?
Then I will take me to the door,
 Nor speak one single word ?"
" No, gentlest ! let thy sister sleep,
 And in her cradle lie—
You must not wake her—lest she weep—
 And come back by-and-by."

SONG.

TELL him that days are past,
 Since first he met me here—
That time went rolling fast
 Whenever he was near.

Tell him that when his eyes—
   I'll love him better then—
Shall see me in the skies,
   I'll never weep again!

Tell him that Luna leads
   The same dear stars that shone
Upon our dew-lit meads,
   When we were all alone!

Tell him that when my heart
   Shall rock his head again,
That we no more shall part,
   And he will love me then.

Tell him—thy wings are fleet—
   The sands are running fast—
That as our first was sweet,
   Shall be our very last.

Tell him—thy wings are fleet—
   And, oh! his heart is true!
Tell him that we shall meet
   Again—thank God!—Adieu!

SONG.

Tell her she need not weep—
   I may not come again—
The vows she would not keep,
   Are falser now than then.

Tell her that too much joy—
　　A theme but seldom sung—
Will soon, like grief, destroy
　　The heart she would have wrung!

Tell her she need not yearn
　　For one she would not know—
The heart that wounds, must learn
　　" To feel another's wo !"

Tell her she need not pine—
　　A few short rolling years
Will bring me unto mine,
　　To wipe away my tears!

Tell her to wipe her eyes,
　　And heed not what they say—
Tell her to hush her sighs,
　　And smile for one away.

Tell her that when we meet,
　　That each one's saddened heart
Will more than gladly beat,
　　To know we were apart!

Tell her that what she was—
　　If once her heart was given—
And may be yet, alas!
　　Hath vanished into heaven!

Tell her without my soul
　　Shall leave my burning breast—
That—then—Adieu!—console
　　Her with eternal rest.

9

TO MY MOTHER.

WRITTEN BEYOND THE MOUNTAINS.

My mother! in this shade where I recline,
  Thou look'st upon me as I am—
The thoughts which now possess me, are as thine,
  And every storm lies sweetly calm.

Thy sunshine is shut from me, as the day
  By midnight!—tears hang from mine eyes
To know that thou art absent and away,
  Thou wall around my paradise!

Oh, mother! art thou not that precious light
  Which shuts out chaos from my soul?
What need have I of sunshine or delight,
  If thou art near me to console?

Thou art, dear mother! as a branching tree,
  And I beneath thee as a lamb—
The winds may blow—they conquer thee—
  And every storm lies sweetly calm.

I am, dear mother! as a beech in spring,
  And thou around me as a vine—
Thine arms brood o'er me like the dove's soft wing,
  To shade me from the hot sunshine.

I am, dear one ! a spark of thine own light,
   And thou the vernal sun that glows ;
When thou dost shine, there is no more of night,
   And life is love without its woes.

I am, as 'twere, a garden, wherein grows
   Uncounted flowers beneath thy sun—
Thou art the spring-tide, I, the stream that flows
   To water all life's posies one by one.

I am, dear parent ! as a fertile field
   Producing fruits of sweetest taste ;
And with thy light a thousand kinds can yield—
   Without it—but a barren waste !

Rejoice, my mother ! for the time is come
   When I shall see thee as thou art—
The same dear parent of my native home—
   And kiss and press thee to my heart.

HYMN TO DEATH.

What man is he that liveth and shall not see death?—*Psalms*, 89 : 48.

Oh ! would it not be joy to lie
Beneath some green arcade and die,
   Where birds are singing loud ;

And shun the deep unfathomed wave,
Nor go down to the silent grave
    Beneath Death's awful cloud.

And would it not be joy to rest
My worn out heart on mother's breast,
    In some fair rosy bower;
And sport awhile beneath the shades,
And listen to the rude cascades,
    And linger for an hour.

And would it not be bliss unknown
To lie down with my bosom's own,
    On some unclouded night;
And drink His dear redeeming love
In ardour shed from heaven above,
    When stars are shining bright.

And would it not be joy to know
That God shall lift my soul from wo,
    When these young eyes are dim;
And leave its cold, wan mansion here,
As winter leaves the willow sere,
    And take it unto Him.

Then murmur not—nor weep—nor sigh—
For death itself shall one day die,
    When God's blest Shiloh comes
To build up Salem's tottering towers,
And crush the Gentile's haughty powers,
    And take us to our homes.

TO MY SISTER,

ON HEARING THAT SHE HAD BORNE TWINS.

Thou hast a rich world around thee.—*Felicia Hemans.*

My sister! what a deep and joyous thing
  It is, to bear two pledges at one birth—
Like two sweet notes from one melodious string,
  To make me happy on a distant earth.
And now, dear sister! soaring on the wing
  Of transport—loving far too deep for mirth—
Fain would my spirit brood upon thy twins—
Two miniatures of life without its sins,

My heart is as a mountain set on fire,
  Which melts into its centre all unseen—
A shrine burnt down amid its own desire,
  To live without enjoying what hath been!
A thing all labouring, but shall never tire,
  That flags for moments to revive again—
Whose unconsuming core shall always burn,
Till life's bright spark shall unto God return.

My heart is as a lyre of many strings,
  Which shall be mute till struck by thy dear hands—
When I shall brood beneath my mother's wings—
  Which none can do upon those distant lands!
9 9

It is, as 'twere, a fount of many springs—
   A thousand streams set over golden sands—
And that which thou wouldst have or sweet or sour,
The same is at thy will this precious hour.

My sister! my dear sister! if my tears
   Are tests of my affections, call me kind !
They flow as if I had ten thousand cares
   To root from out a long-distracted mind !
My life then, after all, is but the years
   Of childhood, which now makes me unresigned
To live from home—whereat my youth was spent—
The four-and-twentieth year of sweet content.

I feel that thou art happy with the rest
   Of those who love me—those who have been dear
To my existence—they, no doubt, are blest—
   While thou art now baptizing with a tear
The two young flowers that bloom upon thy breast—
   Like dew-drops upon lily-bells,—for fear
That some dark angel from among the dead
May fan his icy wings above their head !

My sister ! knowing that my bleeding heart
   Is poured out over thee with many tears !
And feeling that our homes are far apart,
   I charge you, when you think upon the years
That thus have borne me, say,—but do not start—
   He trod his untried pathway without fears ;
And know, that though my feet may cross the sea,
I will from that far land return to thee.

SONG.

Though the rose of my Eden is blasted,
  And the bloom of my youth must decay ;
Though the hopes that we nurtured are wasted,
  And the spring-time has faded away ;
Though the pinion that bound us, must sever,
  And the spring-time to winter be changed ;
Though my heart shall lie bleeding forever,
  Yet, my soul shall not wander estranged.

Though the rock of my fortress is shivered,
  And the star of my glory gone down ;
Though my life to regret be delivered,
  And the pain cause me often to frown ;
Though the eyes that beheld thee, are weeping,
  And my barque cast to flinders shall lie ;
From the grave where my pleasure is sleeping—
  There shall rise one to heaven on high.

Though the heart that was pinioned for glory,
  Be disturbed by the taunts of the vile,
And the hardness of *thine* make it sorry—
  Yet, it never shall break all the while !
Though the thoughts of thy coolness may fret me,
  And the hopes that adored thee be vain ;
Yet, my soul shall revere—nor forget thee—
  And hope still to meet thee again.

BREATHINGS OF THE SOUL.

If a man die, shall he live again?—Man of Uz.

Lord! in the shadow of thy wings,
Bowed in the light of heavenly things—
Fostered by thy redeeming care,
And knowing what thy glories are ;
Let me not ask of thee in vain,
Shall not my spirit live again ?

Lord! would it not be joy to me,
To know that it shall dwell with thee,
And all the kindred of its love,
In that bright holy land above ?
For then these questionings were vain—
Shall not my spirit live again ?

Are not my parents to be known
In that bright region round the throne ?
Are not my brothers to be there ?
And all my sisters as they are ?
And are they not with thee to reign ?
Shall not my spirit live again ?

For, if the Lord's disciples knew
Both Moses and Elias too,
When on the mountain they were seen,
As if they had familiar been ;
Why should these yearnings be in vain ?
Shall not my spirit live again ?

Lord ! if the Shiloh had not died,
And if my soul were satisfied;
And if it were ordained to live
By any thing this world could give ;
I then might ask of thee in vain,
Shall not my spirit live again ?

But seeing that it cannot fill,
And knowing that it hungers still
For that which is to angels given,
To know the mysteries of heaven ;
And feeling that to yearn is pain—
I know that it shall live again.

STANZAS FOR MUSIC.

Oh ! when we remember, with painful delight,
    The days that were brightest are gone,
And look back again unto scenes that were bright,
    As one that must linger alone ;
We think how we garnered those treasures of love,
    When days that we valued were bright,
As tones softly borne far away from the dove,
    And seek them again with delight.

The bright crystal waters whose gushings were first
    The soft tones that startled my ear,
Are borne far away from the place where they burst,
    And no one remains now to hear !

And while we remember how often we met
  In dews that were sent from on high,
As one that resumes her again, with regret,
  The soft harp that caused her to sigh ;

We feel that existence belongs to the past,
  And cling unto hopes that remain ;
And mend every harp-string, though breaking as fast,
  But never shall strike them again !
And thus, only left with affection, forlorn,
  We sigh all alone like the dove
That hastens away from her nest but to mourn,
  And die for the loss of her love !

SONG OF THE POET TO HIS HARP.

Farewell, harp ! Oh ! fare thee well !
  Thou shalt hang upon the willow !
Though thou hast been like the shell
  In its sea-tones o'er the billow—
    Fare thee well !
Thou hast soothed me o'er the mountains,
  Thou hast saved me by the sea ;
Thou hast filled me when the fountains
  All were dry—fare well to thee !

Farewell, harp ! Oh ! fare thee well !
  Thou hast been my solace ever ;
And thy dear kind notes shall dwell
  In my bosom's home forever—
    Fare thee well.

Thou hast taught my soul in sorrow
  To resolve its woes in thee,
That my hopes might be to-morrow
  Brighter still—fare well to thee!

Farewell, harp! Oh! fare thee well!
  Now thy silver chords are broken!
Though my soul doth love thee well,
    All my vows are quickly spoken—
      Fare thee well!
Thou hast made me smile in sadness,
  And my hopes have been to be
In thy name redeemed to gladness,
    As in youth—fare well to thee!

Farewell, harp! Oh! fare thee well!
  Years are gone since thou wert keeping
All my dark locks damp to tell
    Why my soul was doomed to weeping—
      Fare thee well!
Now thy sea-born tones are dying
  On my heart-strings doomed to be
As yon sea-bird sick with flying
    From its shore—fare well to thee!

SONG OF THE MAIDS OF TEXAS.

Awake, love, awake ! for the morning is nigh,
And the sunbeams are bright in the vault of the sky—
The trumpet is heard by the isles of the sea,
Then awake, love, awake ! for my soul is with thee !
The roses are wet with the dews of the night,
And the day-dawn is crowning the hills with delight ;
The roebucks are making their tracks in the sand,
" *And the voice of the turtle is heard in our land.*"

Awake, love, awake ! for the dews of the morn
Are dashed from the boughs by the sound of the horn—
The autumn is gone, and the winter is past,
And the ring-doves are heard in the valleys at last ;
The rose-buds are bright in the light of the dew,
And the sage-bells are booming with nectar for you ;
The cymbal-bee drinks from the chalice at hand,
" *And the voice of the turtle is heard in our land.*"

Awake, love, awake ! for the young fawns are nigh,
And the last star is gone from its home in the sky—
The lily-bells shine in the valleys below,
And the sweet-william shakes by the foot of the roe ;
The snow-pigeon hies from the hill-tops to feed,
And the blackbirds are singing their songs in the mead—
Awake, love, awake ! for my heart and my hand,
" *For the voice of the turtle is heard in our land.*"

THE MOTHER'S SONG

AT THE GRAVE OF HER CHILD.

As the savage makes his tread
  In the mire that turns to stone,
That shall last when he is dead,
  And his children all are gone !
As the foot-print shall be there,
  When the type shall be apart—
So the waves of Time shall wear
  Thee but deeper in my heart !

If the vaulted void be nigh,
  And you cannot hear its moan,
Let the tempest sweep it by,
  And the cavern may be known !
As the storm can only lead
  To the sunless depths below,
So, the region of the dead
  May be gathered from this wo !

As the miner takes the stone
  In its brightness from the earth,
And preserves it as his own
  In his casket for its worth ;
As he wears it on his breast
  As he took it from the sod,
So, my baby takes her rest
  In the bosom of her God.

NEAH-EMATHLAH.

He knew himself a villian—but he deemed
The rest no better than the thing he seemed:
Lone, wild, and strange, he stood alike exempt
From all affection and from all contempt.—*Byron's Corsair*

When Neah-Emathlah was captured, during the recent difficulties with the Creek Indians, the worrior-boy of his heart was also taken; when his son was brought into his presence bound, the old man was very much affected, and betrayed his regard for him—for it was supposed that they would both be shot— and requested that, whatever death he might die, he would fain that his son might live; and looking his enemies full in the face, he told them that he wished to raise his son to fight them, as *he* had fought old Hickory. They were both liberated and taken to Arkansas.

No, paleface! thou shalt expect the tears
  That the father sheds for his dying son!
But the spring dries up after many years,
  And, from these old eyes there shall fall not one!
I have heard thee say that my death was nigh!
That my tribe must *fall!*—that my son shall *die!*
I can only say, for my warrior-love,
Oh! white man! slay not my Eagle-Dove!

The few short years that you rob from me,
  Shall pass like the winds on the raging floods!
But the sudden fall of my son shall be
  As the mighty oak in the silent woods!

And the tears shall fall for his dearest sake,
As the frightened dew when the branches shake
By the sudden sound of my warrior-love—
Oh! white man! slay not my Eagle-Dove!

The poplar stands by the river tall,
   But the giant oak makes the greatest sound ;
And the aged tree may expect to fall
   When his branches shed all their leaves around !
But the sound shall come from the rolling seas,
And the winds shall moan through the forest trees ;
And the voice shall say, for my warrior-love—
Oh! white man! slay not my Eagle-Dove!

I seek not life for my soul to move,
   But the warrior-boy that his father loves,
Is the first-born child of his mother's love,
   And the tallest roe of the Eagle-Doves !
If the bitterest death that my life can give,
Be enough for his—let the young boy live !
If my bleeding heart can suffice to prove—
Oh! white man! slay not my Eagle-Dove!

I know not why that my early death
   Should deter my tale—for the deed is done !
I was once along on this very path,
   And perceived three babes in the woods alone !
I threw them up in the air for life,
And caught them all on my pointed knife—
The *knife* that now would avenge my love—
Oh! white man! slay not my Eagle-Dove!

Oh! who can find for my spirit rest,
   As it passed away with the dying child ?

For the dagger met with its tender breast,
  As it gently looked in my face and smiled!
And, from that sad day, when alone, for years,
I have wept my soul into burning tears!
And, for all these things, thou hast bound my love—
Oh! white man! slay not my Eagle-Dove!

I have bent my bow on the milky swan,
  As she skimmed along o'er the breasted lake;
I have pierced her mate as he wandered on
  O'er the bristled isles of the reedy brake;
But the look that came from the dying child,
As it gently gazed in my face and smiled—
Is upon me still—on my warrior-love—
Oh! white man! slay not my Eagle-Dove!

The turtle hies to her cedar nest,
  And the roebuck wanders from hill to hill;
And the eagle ascends to the sun to rest,—
  But the same deep pangs are my portion still!
For the valley-paths where the infant smiled,
And the awful look of the dying child,—
Are upon me still—on my warrior-love—
Oh! white man! slay not my Eagle-Dove!

Oh! think not, *man!* that my heart is free
  From the iron cares that corrode the breast!
I am fastened here, like an inland sea,
  By the stagnant waves of my woes opprest!
I have not one hope that my tongue can tell!
I have only felt that my soul is—*hell!*
I can only feel for my warrior-love—
Oh! white man! slay not my Eagle-Dove!

113

TO MY HARP.

He is made one with Nature; there is heard
His voice in all her music, from the moan
Of thunder to the song of night's sweet bird.—*Adonais.*

HARP of the sunny South! awake! Oh! wake
  The dove-like melodies that suit the soul!
For thou art stricken for affection's sake,
  And sorrow yieldeth unto thy control!
Oh! come unto me from the realms above,
And minister relief for wounded love.

Thou hast been unto me, amid the night,
  As is the bird's songs to the silent woods;
And filled my spirit with diviner light
  Than ever gushed from out the solitudes,
When contemplation lay upon my breast,
And whispered unto life eternal rest.

Thou hast been unto me an infant nursed
  With life's emulging nectar—very deep!
That only not sufficient for its thirst,
  But after filling yields refreshing sleep.
An incense, rising from the fire of love,
That melts away into the heavens above.

10 10

Oh! when the voice of early love was new,
   The bright creations of the soul were deep—
When life was as the rose-buds in the dew,
   And there was nothing here to make me weep ;
Then, thou wert unto me that glorious light
That sets the stars beneath the heavens at night.

The winds were then harmonious in the trees,
   And jocund were the spirits of the air,
That all night long upon the passing breeze
   Were wont to fondle with my tangled hair ;
And now, though still melodious, they are deep,
And, like thy cadence, often make me sleep !

Oh! there are melodies that never die,
   But like the shell-tones of the ocean deep,
They dwell within us, like the parting sigh
   Of those who feel too many pangs to weep !
And pass like land-tones on the foaming sea,
When wave rolls after wave incessantly.

And, when the heavens above were very bright,
   I hung thee gently on the willow tree !
But, when there came no clouds upon my light,
   I could not say that thou wert dear to me !
For thou didst woo me by the gentle streams,
Like one that wooes his first love in his dreams.

And in the sinless play-time of my youth,
   Beneath the oak-trees of my silent home,
When all my spring-tides rolled along as smooth
   As doth the streams into the vales, whilom—
My heart lay calm like some undimpled lake,
Where sleeps the unscared swan beside the brake.

And when the roebucks in the valley reeds,
   Were seen to crop the languid blades at even ;
And when the young fawns danced upon the meads,
   And watched the first-born of the stars in heaven ;
I swung upon the grape-vines by the spring,
And heard the mock-birds in the valleys sing.

And where the willow boughs embraced the brook,
   The ring-doves cooed upon the cedar-trees—
I sate me down with some old favourite book,
   And heard the pine-tops in the passing breeze ;
And when the dews appeared at day's decline,
I did not think them antetypes of mine !

And when my soul was very young, at noon,
   Beneath the oak-trees of my silent hills—
When all the little flowers were up in June,
   I sate me down upon the gentle rills,
And with some author of poetic song,
I felt instinctively my future wrong !

And when, at eventide, the sun was set,
   A thousand rainbow dyes bedecked the boughs—
I felt within me that which haunts me yet,
   And saw prospectively my broken vows !
For such were latent in my silent heart,
That, since, hath torn its very chords apart !

And when alone, since that delightful hour,
   In sickness, when my soul was very faint—
When grief came on me with redoubled power,
   And all life's energies were wont to pant ;
I felt thy voice within my spirit deep,
And laid my hand upon my head to weep !

Harp of the wounded spirit! thou hast been
   The greatest comfort ever mortal tried!
And though such joys can never be again,
   I still will hold thee always by my side!
For when life's sorrows shall have had an end,
I still will own thee as my dearest friend!

Song of the Southern Lyre! though all is lost
   That made life precious—and the day is gone!
And that dear being who was loved the most,
   Has left me sighing in this world alone!
I now must leave thee for the ocean-shell—
Back to thy native heaven again—*Farewell! Farewell!*

MALAVOLTI;

OR,

THE DOWNFALL OF THE ALAMO.

> Lost, lost, forever lost,
> In the wide pathless deserts of dim sleep,
> That beautiful shape.—*Alastor.*

I.

THERE are two bright stars in the clear blue sky,
   And the east looks blue, and the west looks red,
Like the two first tears in an infant's eye,
   Ere the rose-bud hues from its cheeks have fled.
They are rolling down to the dark blue sea,
   As they mount aloft in the concave deep!
They are travelling now from eternity,
   On the deep dark wings of the night to sleep!
They are rising now from the isles of love,
As they twinkle bright in the realms above!
They are wheeling now in the depths of heaven,
On the radiant hues of the vermil even!
For their tones are soft as the falling dews,
As an angel walks on the rainbow-hues!
And the aspen light of the eastern gloam
Shines brighter now than the brightest beam.
For the last bright steps of the day is fled,
And the stars are glad that they shine in stead,—
But the songs in heaven are joyous still,
For the morning laughs on the jocund hill.

II.

But away in the field afar,
Malavolti looks at the morning star!
He looks at the star for the face of one,
Who shall meet him there ere the day is done.
He looks at the star with the eyes of love,
As it twinkles bright in the realms above;
And his heart beats quick, and his eyes are wet,
For his soul must part from his Lena yet!
And he lifts his hands up to heaven in prayer—
But he sighs, *Amen!*—for the maid is there!

III.

Her eyes were bright with melody,
   'Neath that dark fringe which hangs above,
   Like heaven's pavilion guarding love;
And when her dark melodious eye
   Illumed her bright cherubick thought,
   It seemed as if by lightnings caught,
And tears came out like clouds on high!

IV.

He listened to her gentle strain,—
   It thrilled him like an angel's voice!
And when she lisped the theme again,
   It made his very heart rejoice.
The zephyrs combed her tangled hair,
Disheveled round her bosom bare,
As if some spirit lingered near,
To see her smile and shed a tear—
Like those upon her eyelids bright,
Like scattered stars through clouds at night,

That made his bosom overflow,
Which proves all weeping is not wo—
As evening's dewy mantle gray
Comes down from heaven on parting day.

V.

Her tranquil eyes were brighter far
Than evening's first-born, twilight star,
And shed, amid those lustres bright,
A more celestial, heavenly light,
Which shows how much above the skies
Is love, when seen in woman's eyes.
Her cloudy lashes' velvet fringes,
    Through which her spirit lightened oft,
And caught her eyelids' snowy hinges,
    And made her rosy cheeks so soft ;
That turned her eyes like wild gazelles,
Like dew-drops on the lily-bells ;
And like the dangling muscadine
    Upon the placid waters near,
Or angels over truth divine
    To wipe away each falling tear,—
They languid seemed above each lid,
That kept but half their spirit hid,
And beamed beneath each silken lash,
As lightnings when they gently flash ;
As her white bosom heaved beneath,
As if her sighs could conquer death !
And over which her teeth were set.
And over which her lips were met,
With heaven's celestial nectar wet.

VI.

Her clustering locks, voluptuously,
    Around her panting bosom lay,
And floated with such modesty,
    That guile was turned away.
The winds were through her tresses flowing,
And roses on her cheeks were blowing,
As beautiful as ever shed
Their hues upon a violet bed.
And when her arms, distinctly bare,
But shone beneath her glossy hair,
And all their azure veins were flowing
Above her ruby rivers glowing,
Like vermeil lines bestreaking roses,
Before the dawn of beauty closes—
They looked more like an angel's fair,
Than any painting richly rare,—
As gently rounding, tapering, chaste,
As any antique beauty's waist,
As if some angel's hand had traced
Each tender line—each azure shade—
Before her heavenly form was made

VII.

Her eyes were dazzling softly bright,
Beneath her eyelids' solemn light,
So that her deep, expressive mind
Kept half her spirit's hues behind,
In that fond spark that lurked below,
Which made her very beauty glow,
Whose virgin meekness gave her eyes
The modest hue of twilight skies ;

For roses that are wet with dew,
Shine brightest under heaven of blue,
As beauty in her early years
Looks brightest when beheld in tears.
Her polished brow, above her eyes,
Her spirit's bright melodious sphere,
      Above her purple orbits' roll,
Was brighter far than pearly skies,
In summer, when the sun doth rise
As cloudless and as clear away
As ever shone the brightest day;
      And when her flashing spirit stole
From out her cloudy fringe above,
And told how eloquent was love —
It gave her such divine delight
That thought was drowned beneath the light.

VIII.

And he clasped her there to his beating breast,
    As he wiped the tears from her weeping eyes!
But another stole from her soul's behest,
    As her spirit burst with her pent up sighs!

" Oh, God!" said she, "must the loving part?"

And the maiden wept, and her lover sighed,
    For the damsel swore she would be his bride —

" Then take this image and wear at thy heart!
In the battle, on earth, on the land, or the sea,
Oh! forget not the pledge that is given to thee!"

11

IX.

And such her early love had given
To win him from the world to heaven—
A deep Promethean agony,
    Whose bright delirium warmed her heart!
And worked upon each bitter sigh,
    Till every string was torn apart!
In conquering life's autumnal woes,
    The heart gets older than the head—
The mind may war with beauty's blows,
    When every thrill lies cold and dead!
The boundless mind may widely range,
But hearts, once broken, never change,
But fettered fast, must, beating still,
Be made the brunt of every ill!
Till too much sorrow, in the calm
Of suffering, brings its own soft balm.
For passing life can never prove
The real worth of by-gone love,
Though fraught with unrequited grief,
And pangs that cannot find relief.
Yet, thinking we may be again,
And how much better could have been,
Will sometimes cancel deep distress,
And charm away life's bitterness ;
Till walking Death's unlighted shore,
We feel that we shall be no more,
Beneath those dark, accustomed shades,
Beyond which this existence fades,
Till borne to sweeter climes above
By God's all-righteous dove.

X.

The herald dove returned no more,
That died upon his native shore !
And why should Malavolti start,
When one embrace had soothed her heart ?
Ah ! better had she ne'er have been !
But she shall never weep again !
Such tears cannot alloy that grief,
For which there can be no relief !

XI.

'Twas not his velvet verdure bright,
　　That rivalled green Idalia's bowers ;
And not his starry spangled night,
That gave her heart such sweet delight,
　　　When evening's freshening gale
　　　Beguiled her soul with fragrant flowers,
　　　As those along Thessalia's vale,
As bright as Coromandal's coast,
Or all that India prizes most ;
And not for his pearly softness streaming
From silver brooklets brightly beaming—
For she shall live on earth no more,—
But more than Peru's gaudy lore !
When he besieged her father's fold,
The tender sire was growing old !
Who shed, alas ! ten thousand tears.
To wash away his bitter cares !
To know that she was torn apart
To gratify an alien's heart !
He heard them read her last demise,
And saw them close her dying eyes !

And darken that fast-fading light
That gleamèd upon his aged sight!
But there are joys like heaven below,
And many sweets we never know!
And there are thoughts that never die,
Though clouds obscure our brightest sky,
A joy that grief can never bind,
    The dearest friend when others flee;
And though our hearts may break, the mind,
    The only portion truly free—
Will never lead our sorrows blind.

XII.

But she who bore her guilt, when none
Would heed her sighs—was dead and gone!
She saw her die! and, at her death,
She would have bartered her own breath,
Had she but known it could been given
As current pay to God in heaven!
The one that loved her from her birth,
The dearest friend she had on earth!
Three little moons had passed away,
Her soul got restless—could not stay—
And flew to that divine abode,
Where mortal feet have never trode!

XIII.

Nay! was not Malavolti left?
Of every friend on earth bereft?
When every bliss that passion gave,
Consigned to lay him in the grave?
But there are hopes beyond this wo,
That mortal man shall never know,

Till crowned amid that heavenly bliss
Which never grew from worlds like this.
And Lena was divinely fair,
But he had swapped her for despair !
Suffice it, then, they had to part,
The very thing that broke her heart !
The chain that love had for them wrought,
Had links beyond the reach of thought !
But every link was broke in twain,
And never more shall weld again !
And lower, now, than native rose,
Her bosom sleeps in sweet repose !
As fair as that sepulchral stone,
That, once neglected, lies alone !
For when her tender vitals froze,
And mocked each lid's imperfect close,
As evening when she seeks the west,
And shuts the gates of day to rest,
With half her radiant hues behind—
Thus passed away her tranquil mind !
And those fond hues that dyed her face,
Where purple tints had taken place,
As round her lips—beneath her eyes—
The deadly blood had left its dyes—
The darker grew the nearer death,
And knew no vitalizing breath ;
For icy Death had chilled forever
    The ruddy stream that moved her heart,
As winter clogs the limpid river,
    Though both its shores are wide apart.

XIV.

He dug his heart a cruel ditch,
Because his parents made him rich !

11 11

And whensoe'er he plead his cause,
He quoted wealth in every clause !
And though he sowed his seeds with art,
Yet, thorns imparadised his heart !
For who, that leaves the tares to grow,
But reaps his harvest all of wo ?
The dove that pecks the frugal hand,
    That would bestow her fledglings food,
Must fly away from land to land,
    To gather that not half so good !
But no one fed that hungry dove,
Till angels took her home above !

XV.

The milky moon was sadly bright,
And shone above that tropic night,
Like beauty half suppressed by fright.
    He lay upon his lonely bed—
The deep blue tears were in his eyes,
As damply blue as April skies.
    He laid his hand upon his head,
As Cynthia through his lattice shone,
Like tender flesh through maiden's zone—
Nor had he closed his eyes, alas !
For fear that Lena's form might pass—
That fearful thing he wished to see,
    But knew not how she should appear,
For those who leave eternity,
    Are ghosts above their narrow sphere !
And had he known what phantom dress
That night had decked her loveliness,
Her lovely form had shocked him less.

XVI.

He rose.   " Behold that form," said he,
" Beneath yon weeping willow tree !"

And raised the window—moved each blind—
   And when he heard it gently screak,
He thought, in his distracted mind,
   He heard his dying Lena's shriek !
But, with his most determined art,
He only heard his beating heart.

XVII.

The tresses on her neck were flowing,
   That shone beneath her glossy hair
Like earth below when skies are snowing—
   For darkness made her more than fair.
She waved her hand—but nothing said—
   And Malavolti would have spoken—
But he was silent as the dead,
   As thus his very heart was broken :

XVIII.

" The wretch that clothes himself with spoils,
A robber meets for all his toils !
That takes away and sells the whole,
To Death, his body—Hell, his soul !
The heart that wounds another's breast
The very one he could have blest,—
In wounding, seeks his own unrest !
The blind that cannot misery see,
Are not alone from misery free !

The hand that robs existence, fain
 Would guard defenceless virtue best—
Nay ! murderer ! thou art still the pain
 Of those whom hell would not molest !
And every shock that chilled my clay
Shall damn thee in thy last decay !
The melancholy heavens above
Have registered thy faithless love !
But murmur not—thy pangs are sure—
For thou shalt find no earthly cure !
But seething fires shall melt in vain
Thy soul enchained in hell again !
For thou shalt there remain immured,
To tell thee what my soul endured !
Thou hast my generous hope denied,
And hell shall all thy pangs deride !
The dullest thing that crawls this earth,
 Is happier now than thou shalt be !
For thou wert round my bosom girth,
 And thus shall hell encompass thee !
The heart that robs another's weal,
 And feeds upon exultant joy,
Shall smite itself with poisoned steel,
 And never more itself destroy !
Nor e'en through time's forbearance heal,
But twice ten thousand torments feel !
And every thing it values most,
Shall nothing seem—till ever lost !
The eyes betray, when lips are hushed,
 More real love than words express ;
And hearts divulge, when cheeks are flushed,
 More perfect love than saints possess.
One single, soft, compressive shake,
Will make more tender heart-strings ache,

And one fond look from virtue, teach,
 In stronger eloquence than speech,
Though gently suasive, sweetly taught,—
More social bliss than human thought,
 At loftiest height, can ever reach.
But heed thee not another's voice,
For thou shalt never more rejoice !
Though Lena's soft, salubrious breath
Is hushed amid the waves of death !
For those auspicious hopes, so vain,
Shall never touch her heart again !
But, like her own, thy fate shall be
 To die almost as desolate !
And that which thou shalt long to see,
 Shall pleasure bring—but come too late !
And earth shall win thee many woes !
For wretched men are doomed to blows,
Sometimes from friends as well as foes !
And thou shalt recollect, alas !
The bitter things that come to pass !"

XIX.

And thus she warned that restive wight,
And thus she spoke that sheeny night !
As Luna's fair, but tranquil face,
In heaven's blue concave left her trace,
While by her side two stars were seen —
But what could this long vigil mean ?
 And she is gone into heaven again,
 And never, never shall he, in vain,
 Behold her beauty more !

But as she hath spoken shall be his pain,
    Till the grave shall cover him o'er !
And her frosty cheeks, and her hands so wet,
And her icy lips with his own that met ;
And her sylph-like beauty that summer night,
And her downy steps that were lovingly light,—
Are gone again into heaven above,
To answer against him with consummate love.

XX.

The mountain Oread lists awhile,
To bear her voice away from guile !
The water Nymphs may lave their hair,
But Lena's form shall not be there
To lend her sweet Etrurian art
To soften Malavolti's heart !
For now her soft melodious breath
Is hushed beneath the waves of death !
And thus with guilt before—behind—
He rushed away from human kind.

XXI.

He lived alone five hills between,
Whose sunny peaks are always green,
For while they glistened high with snow,
The roses blossomed bright below,
The birds were on their branches singing,
And fountains from their basis springing,
That eddied near, but onward run,
Till many first, were, lastly, one.

And over these celestial waters
 The exile shed his daily tears!
And mourned, alas! like Zion's daughters,
 When captive in their earlier years!
The valley spread its waving green,
And mantled every hill between.
And Gilead balms, perfumed the air,
But Ishmael's sons were wanting there.
No fragments there from ancient walls,
But flindered rocks from waterfalls—
An elegance that art survives—
The finest touch the painter gives.
Though Jacob's well cannot be seen,
 Where Shiloh saw Samaria's daughter,
Adown each emerald hill between,
 Five fountains from their crystal water,
Till all uniting, eddying, make
One gentle, deep, unruffled lake,
That, like man's life must onward go,
And end—but where—we do not know.

XXII.

He raised her—she was cold as ice—
And prest her to his bosom twice!
For she had scaped Ozemba's power,
And had been captive till that hour!
And when she called Ozemba's name,
A tremor ran through all her frame!
The Sachem who had bound her hands,
And torn her from her father's lands!
And while her fearful body shivered,
The exile's lips with vengeance quivered!
And Malavolti thus replied:

The wilderness, my love! is wide—
The lion, though innured to wrath,
Will never cross Naymoyah's path"—

" But stay," said she, " his iron teeth,
The bright uplifted sword beneath,
His snow-white talons, newly bare—
Could give me no unkind despair ;
But doom'd Ozemba's wife to be,
First made me from his presence flee !"

And Malavolti's cheek grew pale
To hear Naymoyah's wonderous tale !

" The lion's eyes may meet thine own,
But he shall drop to earth like stone !
And thou shalt thread thy finger's through
                His darkly flowing mane !
And on his cheeks thy tresses strew,
And feel, for fear, no inward pain !
For nought that lives—that would not die—
Shall look upon Naymoyah's eye,
        While she retains her purity.

' Away ! Naymoyah cried,' my heart shall bleed !
        He rides upon his snowy steed !"

But his thundering hoof, and his whirlwind breath
Shall never return from the valley of death !
And lo ! he descends from the back of his steed,
To claim his Naymoyah or die there indeed !

XXIII.

He drew his hatchet—raised his knife—

" Now, paleface ! give me back my wife !"

He clenched his teeth—his lips were parted—
His eyeballs from their sockets darted!

"Halt, warrior! *halt!*" Naymoyah said,—
Strike, Malavolti! strike him dead!"

"This soul," said he, "can never die!
And by yon big light in the sky"—

"*Strike, Malavolti! strike!*" she said,—
And Malavolti struck him dead!

XXIV.

They mounted his charger, Naymoyah before,
The white noble steed that was standing on shore—
And galloped away into other dark lands,
With guilt in his bosom, and blood on his hands!
And long shall they value the fast flying horse
That bore them away from their enemy's course;
But he who is holding his dark flowing mane,
Shall never come back with Naymoyah again!

XXV.

And away in the field afar,
The warrior looks at the western star—
He looks at the star for the face of one
Who shall meet him there ere the day is done!
He looks at the star with the eyes of love,
As it twinkles bright in the realms above;
And his heart beats quick, and his eyes are wet,
For his soul must part from the maiden yet!
And his eyes are dim with the tears they shed,
As he weeps for the living, and sighs for the dead!
12

And he lifts his hands up to heaven in prayer— .
But he sighs, *Amen !*—for the maid is there !

XXVI.

And he clasped her there to his beating breast,
 As she wiped the tears from the warrior's eyes ;
But another stole from his soul's behest,
 As her spirit burst with her pent up sighs !

" Oh, God !" said she, " must the loving part ?
Then take this image and wear at thy heart !
In the battle, on earth, on the land, or the sea,
Oh ! forget not the pledge that is given to thee !"

And the maiden wept, and the warrior sighed !
For the damsel swore she would be his bride—
But his doom was sealed when his Lena died !

XXVII.

And the maiden stood by the river's side,
 With her rosy cheek on her lily hand ;
And the tears fell down from her soul so wide,
 That they seemed like dew on the silver sand !
And her eyes were bent on the dewy shore,
 For the flowers of earth were the books she read—
And upon them there would her spirit pore,
 Till the last bright star from the heavens had fled
And, as one forlorn, like the mateless dove,
 Would she all day long for her lover sigh !
As she cast her eyes up to heaven above,
 When the stars came out on the clear blue sky.

And with solemn sighs would she hum the song
   That her lover sang when her hopes were bright;
But we need not say that he did her wrong—
   For he came not back to her home that night!

XXVIII.

And the warrior lay by the river deep,
Where the thunders cradled his soul to sleep;
And he dreamed he saw in the realms of heaven,
A thousand stars from their centres driven!
And descending on through eternal years,
With his spirit scathed by the rolling spheres!
He was borne away on a sea-sick cloud,
Where the thunders pawed on his soul aloud,
To an ice-berg car in the raging sea,
Where he tossed from Time to Eternity!
And in whose deep gulf he was doomed to lie
With the living death that shall never die!
When an angel rose from the coral caves,
And scattered pearl on the chiming waves!
For her hands had culled from the ruby cells
The richest gem that in ocean dwells!
And she sate her down on the distant shore,
And attuned her harp to the wild sea's roar—
For the song she sang was the one that burst
On his very soul when she met him first!

" By the light that falls on the foaming sea,
Oh! maiden bright! come away to me!
By the perjured vows that the maiden bore,
Oh, Spirit! come from that blessed shore!
By the torment felt by the damned in hell,
Oh, Spirit! come from that coral cell!

By the sorrows known to the soul in wo,
Oh, Spirit ! come to my home below !
By the many prayers of the deathless dead,
Oh, Spirit! come to my sinking head !"

And he cried aloud for that angel's hand,
But she sate and smiled on the coral strand.
And around him clung, with an ivy grasp,
A huge sea-snake which he could not grasp !
And its crunching coil on his writhing frame,
Like the scorpion girt by the lashing flame—
Ten thousand times round his body clung,
And impierced his soul with its forked tongue !
When, at last, she rose from the sacred spot,
And ascended on—for she heeded not—
Where he never more shall behold his bride—
For his doom was sealed when his Lena died !
And no aid shall come till his chains are riven
By the mightiest King in the realms of heaven.

XXIX.

And away they march, with their Tyrant clad
    In the rich array of his snow-white steed,
As his voice breaks forth from the music sad,
    " *To war ! to war ! for the foe shall bleed !*"
And the lance was levelled—the bows were bent—
    And the Tyrant dashed on his fiery steed—
With the spear and the gorget, away they went
    For the Alamo with the lightning's speed !

        And they march along
        To the glorious song
        Of the triumph yet to be ;

And the flashing sword,
  At the Tyrant's word,
Shines bright for the victory.

And the trampling feet
  To the music sweet,
Are heard in the field afar,
  As the trumpet noise
  Of the Tyrant's voice
Breaks forth from the hills, " *To war !*"

And the march is slow
  As the mighty flow
Of a river deep and bright,
  As the charger's bound
  Makes the woodlands sound
Like an earthquake born at night !

And the march is slow
  To the music low,
As the fiery charger flings
  Off the volleying bound
  Of the earthquake sound
From the hoofstroke where he springs.

And the woodland birds,
  And the countless herds,
Are escaping away before ;
  As the trooping host
  In the dust are lost,
As they march to the widening shore.

And the Tyrant mailed
  By the lancers trailed,

Is curving the sun-clad hill,
    As he leads them on
    From the victory won,
Where the casque shines brighter still.

    And the lancers dashed,
    As the armour flashed,
On the green of the plain below ;
    And the army sighed
    When the Tyrant cried,
" A charge, brave men ! for the foe !"

" A charge ! for destruction is all for the few !
    A charge for your Liberty ! Freedom ! or death !"

They grapple !—they struggle !—they bleed ! but the crew
    That remains are now losing their breath !
The sabre, all dinted, lies swimming in gore,
And the dying are crawling the vanquishing o'er !
And the thorny walls they were built in vain,
    For he conquers them with his tyrant power !
And the blood is shed, and the brave are slain,
    As he slew them not in another hour.
For the prophecy Texas hath spoken to thee,
Is written in heaven—*that she shall be free !*

XXX.

The morn is broke in the downy east,
    And the bright red star of the dawn is free ;
For the raven descends on the dead to feast,
    And the vulture is whetting his beak by the sea.
They cleave their curve in the charnal air,
    As they circle around on the wayward wind ;
And their fellows glide by the banquet there,

As they rustle their wings to the rest behind.
They are gathering now on the battle plain,
   As they flap their wings on the recent dead,
For they rove about on the tombless slain,
   Like the night seawaves when the day is fled.
And the wolf is fat, and the jackal's cry
   Is heard no more in the forest dim,
For the vulture picks out the soulless eye,
   As they tear him limbless, limb by limb!
But they need not fight, for the flesh is free,
   And their sated gorge should forbid them war—
They should dwell in peace and satiety,
   For the morning breaks on the hills afar.

XXXI.

And the dying lay on the bloody sod,
   Like the lowland reeds when the storm is high!
And their eyes were turned to the throne of God,
   As the good man looks when he comes to die!
And as one lay there on his wounded breast,
   Here, another fell where the foremost led;
And as one lay there on his back to rest,
   Here, the dying leant on the sidelong dead!
And as those who fell in the furious van,
   Were weltering deep in the oozing gore;
So, the rest who followed, were, man to man,
   Seen lying along on the dead before!
And as some were seen lying face to face,
   With their fingers clasped on the recent slain,
So, the steadfast look of the last embrace
   Told all that the soul could express of pain!
And as one lay stretched by his dying steed,

Where his eyeballs glared in his pallid face,
So, another fell like the broken reed,
    When the torrent swells from its native place.
For the brave had died with their cheeks as red
As the crimson gore of the recent dead!
And they passed away with their triumph smile
As fresh as the light of their sun-clad isle.
For the first went off with their lips apart,
As they uttered all for the labouring heart!
And the rest that fell, to the latest gasp,
Held fast to their swords with an iron grasp.
And the eyes that turned to the shining sun,
Seemed to tell high heaven what the foe had done!
And the stern, proud look of the lofty brow,
In the long, deep calm, told the lover's vow!
While around were seen in the looks of some,
The last fond thoughts of their wives at home!
And there stole from one, when his heart was weak,
A half shed tear on his bloody cheek!
And beside were seen, with his sinking head,
    A *man*, who leant on his charger's mane;
And his clotted hair in the blood was red,
    As his hand lay clenched on the slackened rein!
For his soul had left on his pallid cheek
    The last deep thought that to life was given;
But the voice that the living nor dead could speak,
    Is spoken aloud for the brave in heaven.

XXXII.

The moon rose high in the fulgent even,
    And the stars were bright on the silent sea,
When the maiden raised up her hands to heaven,
    And said, " How long will he stay from me ?"

The star-gemmed wings of the night were spread
  Over all high heaven to the farthest skies;
And the wind-stirred grass, from her fawn-like tread,
  Fell down like the tears from her deep blue eyes!
For the foes were slain, and the battle fought,
  And the maiden stood by the river's side—
But the vulture claimed what the maiden sought
  For his doom was sealed when his Lena died!
And she seeks the field for her absent love,
  As she leaves her steps on the silver sand:
But an angel comes from the heavens above,
  And grasps her fast by the lily hand!

"Oh God!" said she, "from the realms on high!
  Then speak to the wretched and let her pass;
Shall the warrior live?—shall the maiden die?"—
  And the Angel said to the maid, "Alas!"

"Oh! speak to my soul, for thy hand is cold,
And thy locks are richer than strans of gold!
Oh! what is the fate of my love to be!
And say, what caused thee to come to me?"

And the spirit raised her hands up to heaven,
And said, "Fond maid! thou shalt hear this even!
  Thy love is dead!—"
           "*For his country's sake?*
  Oh! away, false one! for my heart must break!"

"Nay! arise, fair maiden! and hear me tell,
The warrior's soul's in the depths of hell!"

"*In hell?—did he die on the battle-field?*"

"He died with his blood on his battered shield!

I have come, fair maiden! thy soul to take"—

" *Oh! away, false one! for my heart must break!*"

" Nay, awhile, dear one! thou shalt hear the truth—
I was once like thee, in my sinless youth!
I was fair, like thee, in the hour of trust,
But his heart was false, and my hopes were dust!
I believed him true—was betrayed like thee—
For his smiles were more than the world to me!
I have met thee here for thy soul's own sake"—

" *Oh! away, false one! for my heart must break!*"

" It shall never break on this side the grave!
I have come, fair maiden! thy soul to save!
For the God of light from the heavens above"—

" *Hath sent thee to save?—then redeem my love!*"

" I have watched thee long from the western star—
I have seen thee look at my home afar!
I have heard thee sigh for the wretch in hell!
Where his cursed soul shall forever dwell!
I adored him once, when my youth was love,
But an angel took me to heaven above!
For the very wretch that was bound to thee,
Was the same foul fiend that was false to me!
I have left my home for thy precious sake"—

" *Oh! away, bright one! for my heart must break!*"

XXXIII.

Oh! how happy then was the maiden's flight,
   As the angel's wings to her soul were given ;

As she bathed them there in the sun's pure light,
　Ere she met her God in the realms of heaven!
And she left no trace on the sunny land,
But her sandalled track in the river sand.
For her steps were soft as the frightened fawn,
　When he stamps the dews from the lily-bells—
When he stands afar on the hills at dawn,
　By the reed-isles green where his mother dwells.
But 'tis ever thus with the world below,
There are many sweets—but they pain us so,
That the good all dies just to kill the wo!
But it teaches man that his soul was given
But to win his way from the earth to heaven.

THE END.